Perilous Games

Louise had to discover what secret was shadowing her aged father's life—and free him of that unending nightmare.

Louise had to rescue her handsome, headstrong brother from an amorous involvement that was dragging him down into a quicksand of dishonor and disgrace.

And Louise had to find a way to win the mocking, maddening man she loved, while escaping the clawlike clutches of the lascivious lord she loathed.

The wicked, worldly city of London had become Louise's chessboard—and she dreaded to think what a wrong move might bring . . .

Watch for the forthcoming novel
by Darrell Husted,
in Popular Library editions:

MISS CORDELIA HARLING

A Country Girl

by Darrell Husted

POPULAR LIBRARY • NEW YORK

Published by Popular Library, a unit of CBS
Publications, the Consumer Publishing Division of CBS Inc.

March, 1978

Copyright © 1978 by Darrell Husted

ISBN: 0-445-04186-2

For Mabel Torvie

Chapter 1

At each lurch and bounce of the coach, Louise felt more miserable. She was solidly wedged between two fleshy women, each taking more than her share of the space. She could only sit rigidly upright and stare unhappily in front of her at three amply proportioned gentlemen of middle years, two of whom were loudly snoring. The third was casting appreciative though covert glances at her, and this heightened her unease. Because the weather was nippy, the coach windows had been firmly slammed shut by the formidable woman on her right, and the atmosphere was stiflingly close without being cozy.

Until today, Louise had never been farther than ten miles from Twelve Elms, her father's estate in Sussex, and now here she was on her way to London. It should have been an adventure, but she didn't feel excited—she only felt a vague apprehension and unease, as though she were surrounded by hundreds of little demons, each carrying a different doubt and fear. What would she find in London? Would Charles be easy to trace? Had he come to some harm? Perhaps he was . . . ? She dared not complete the thought, and pushed it away with a shudder.

The woman at her right took this movement as an affront and said testily, "Sorry, indeed, miss, I'm sure, if I'm crowding you."

"Not at all, ma'am. I . . . I . . . simply had a little chill."

The woman gave a grunt that sounded disapproving, adjusted her brown shawl, and settled back into her own thoughts, leaving Louise unhappily to hers.

She could still hear, as clearly as though he were with her, her father's half-strangled voice:

"You must find Charles, you must find what's happened to him. It's been three months . . . it should never have been this long. One month . . . or six weeks . . . but three months . . . too long." His hands fretted with the counterpane as he tried to raise his head to emphasize the urgency of his words. Since his stroke, less than a month ago, his already poor health had deteriorated alarmingly. Louise was frightened at the intensity of his plea. It reinforced her own misgivings about her brother's long absence.

She was confused then, as she had been earlier, about the purpose of her brother's trip. She only knew that it was to perform some commission that her father thought exceedingly important. She remembered her father's brief annual trips to London, made with grim regularity each May, from which he returned dour and unhappy. It always took him several days to regain the calm and kindly, though melancholy, outlook that was habitual to him.

But this year he had not been able to travel. Though not very old, his health had seemed simply to give way beneath some burden and he had sunk under its weight, growing ever weaker.

He had become more worried and fearful as May approached, causing both Louise and Charles—and particularly old Agatha, who had been their nanny and was now the housekeeper—to do all in their power to calm and comfort him. But he would not be comforted. He kept insisting that he must make the trip to London as usual, long after it had become apparent that he was unable to do so. Then one evening he had summoned Charles to the library, and behind closed doors had given him the errand.

Charles had emerged, looking both grave and very excited.

"I'm to go to London," he told Louise, unable to keep the joy out of his voice. "Father says I'm to leave in a week's time." And he grinned.

"Oh, Charles," she said, "what ever shall we do while you're gone? Please be careful."

"Nonsense. I shan't be more than a fortnight. And careful of what? After all, a trip to London isn't that unusual, you know." He swaggered a little, to try to cover his excitement. In fact, a trip to London was very unusual. It was something he had wanted for a long while. Ever since he had been eighteen years old he had been trying to get away from Twelve Elms, to get out into the "world," as he called that space beyond the perimeter of the estate. But he had constantly been frustrated. Most recently he had wanted to join the army to fight against Bonaparte, but his father had refused because there was not enough money to buy him a commission, and he would not permit Charles to go as a common soldier—though he would have been willing enough to do so. Now, at last, he was to get away, though only for a brief while, and even the gravity of his duty could not dampen his excitement.

The brother and sister had been interrupted then by Agatha who, upon being told that Charles was to leave in a week, threw her apron up to her eyes and began to cry.

"But you're not old enough!" she had sobbed. "What can your father be thinking of? I'll go talk to him this minute."

"You'll do nothing of the sort," Charles said, taking her by the arm and brusquely pulling her back into the kitchen. Louise was startled at the angry brutality of his voice. "You'll keep out of this, Agatha. I'm twenty-two years old, and not a baby to be kept in check by nannies."

"Charles—" Louise began, shocked at the cruelty in his voice and the stricken look on old Agatha's face.

"And remember, miss,"—he turned on her—"I'm two years older than you, and will soon be master here. So I advise you not to interfere in what doesn't concern you."

He had stormed out of the house then, leaving the two hurt women huddled together in confusion. Agatha was still sobbing, with her apron to her nose, though now because of her treatment by Charles rather than because of his trip. Louise tried to console her.

"He didn't mean to be unkind, Agatha. Please don't cry, dear . . . there. . . ." and Louise patted her shoulder, which only seemed to make her cry the more.

"What got into him? I've been a mother to him, ever since your own dear mother died. I've treated you both as my own. Now he turns against me. . . ."

"Please Agatha, you know we love you. He didn't mean it. He was just frightened, my dear. . . ."

Eventually her tears had subsided and she

had gone back to her work, though grumbling under her breath.

Charles had stayed out all day, and Louise had not met him again until that evening at dinner, where they and their father were served by a village girl who was overseen by a glacially aloof and markedly wounded Agatha.

Their father, as he had been lately, was pale and withdrawn at the head of the table, picking at his food and saying little. Louise had tried to interest him in the events of the day, and he would respond to her chatter politely and gravely, only to subside again into his own reticence. Charles had uttered nothing but monosyllables, and had gone off alone as soon as he could decently excuse himself.

Later, Louise had searched him out in the library.

"Charles," she had said timidly, "please don't be cross with me and Agatha. We were only worried."

He stiffened, then smiled ruefully.

"I'm sorry, Louise," he had replied. "I was beastly to you both. But I've wanted to get away for so long, and then suddenly, when it seems I have the chance, I just couldn't allow anything to threaten me. I was awful to you. Forgive me. I'll make it up to Agatha somehow."

And he had. The following day he had arisen early and gone out. He returned from the fields with a huge bouquet of daffodils for Agatha. She had resisted initially, but then had given in and soon was responding again to his teasing as though nothing had happened.

When the day came for Charles to leave for London, both Agatha and Louise were standing at the entrance waving good-bye and watching his jaunty departure on old Plato, their chestnut.

Their father had not left his room that morning. The waiting began, and he became more apprehensive and withdrawn. Then there was the morning that Louise had been awakened by a scream from the library. She had rushed downstairs to find the little village girl who helped Agatha sobbing and pointing at what looked like a bundle of old clothes heaped on her father's chair. It was her father, his face grotesquely contorted and his eyes squeezed shut, as though with pain. He was breathing laboriously, and seemed intent on saying something, but no words would come. They had gotten him to his room, and he had not left it since. That was where he had told Louise a few days ago that Charles must be found and the result of the errand learned.

The coach bumped and rattled over an unusually rough spot in the road, awaking one of the snoring gentlemen.

"Wha—wha—are we there?"

"No we are not, sir," replied the woman to Louise's right. "Nor shall we be for another two hours."

The passengers settled down again. The two women wiggled, on either side of Louise, and her admirer across the way seemed to be on the point of winking at her when she quickly looked away.

Two hours. Louise could have wished it were another two weeks. Or two years. The idea of London frightened her, all the more because she was to be met by her aunt—a sour, unaffectionate woman, her father's sister. Louise had only met her once, when she had stayed at Twelve Elms for a month, constantly complaining of the amenities she was lacking in the country that existed at her fingertips in "town." Going to London was bad enough, but having to beg for hospitality made the undertaking even more disagreeable. She had written hastily to her aunt, a widow whose married name was Hartshord, and had not even had the time to wait for a reply. Knowing the value that Mrs. Hartshord put on correctness, Louise realized that this would not set well at all. Ideally she should have made a polite inquiry, waited for an affirmative answer, then written another polite letter accepting her aunt's invitation. But there hadn't been time. The urgency in her father's plea had precluded a long period of correspondence. So now

Louise was to arrive and be met by, no doubt, a very grumpy and supercilious aunt.

When Louise had first learned that her father wished her to search out Charles, she had timidly suggested that perhaps their Aunt Hartshord could make inquiries. Her father had become even more agitated, and had trembled.

"No! Your aunt musn't be told of this! This is our business. . . . Do not tell your aunt. . . ."

"But father," she had timidly asked. "what is it? . . . Can't you let me know? . . ."

"Charles knows what had to be done," was all her father would say, and then he lapsed into a sorrowful and agitated silence.

So she had set about getting ready, mending her few simple dresses and setting the house in order. Then she had departed, with only Agatha to see her to the coach stop and wait tearfully until the large, rumbling conveyance came into sight. With many admonitions to be careful, Agatha had helped her up and had stood clutching her handkerchief to her nose until the coach was out of sight.

Louise had had to squeeze in between the two unfriendly women, who made a great show of finding room for her. She had been sitting there ever since.

The coach's movements became more jerky, and it even stopped a couple of times. By straining a little, Louise could see out the window and remark upon the thickening traffic. She surmised that London must be very near. She knew she was correct when her fellow travelers began to straighten themselves up, the women primping a little, tucking stray locks under their bonnets, and the gentlemen adjusting their cravats and squirming out of their travel-induced lethargy.

"Excuse me, ma'am," Louise said to the woman on her right. "Are we almost there?"

"Almost? Indeed we are there. We have arrived."

As though it dared not contradict her, the coach came to a creaking, rocking stop. In a few minutes the doors were flung open and the passengers began to descend. The two stout women left first, with much agitation and many commands about their luggage. Then Louise was handed down, followed by the three gentlemen. Louise reflected that never had she spent so much time with people for whom she had so little sympathy.

As though they were all genies, they disappeared immediately upon alighting, leaving Louise standing forlornly on the road amidst the bustle of carters and coachmen. Now she truly did feel alone, for nowhere was her aunt to be seen. Furthermore, the bustling men around her were beginning to remark the slender young woman with the black hair, softly curling around her heart-shaped face, and the deep blue, apprehensive eyes fringed with thick lashes. The slight flush that agitation brought to her creamy skin only heightened her appeal. Though she was not aware of her effect on the men watching her, she was sensible that she was in an exposed and very uncomfortable position. She stood between her two shabby trunks and did not know where to turn.

"Ah, there you are," a brusque male voice said.

She looked up at one of the most splendid men she had ever seen. He was tall, had black hair cut low over the forehead, deep brown eyes, and a fine mouth set above a strong chin. He was wearing a coat of plum velvet over black satin breeches. The whole was set off by snowy linen showing at his throat and cuffs. Louise could only gape at him.

"There you are," he repeated in an unfriendly manner. "I thought you had missed the coach, but it seems that your coach was simply late. Your aunt sent me to fetch you." This was all said in the driest possible manner, as though he were delivering a message learned by rote.

"I'm very grateful, sir, that you should have come, for I was feeling frightened and very worried—" Louise began.

"No need for that."—he cut her off. "Where's your servant? Gather her up along with your things and let's be off. Your aunt's waiting for you."

His peremptory manner began to work on her already taut nerves. "I have no servant, sir. I came alone."

"Ah," he said, and raised an eyebrow. "That's a long distance to be traveling without a servant. How ever did you manage?" The question was posed sarcastically.

Louise turned from him in order to gather her wits. She could not understand why this splendid man should feel such animosity toward her. She was not accustomed to anything but kindness from men she met, and had not the weapons to combat hostility. She felt near to tears.

"I . . . I . . . managed very well, sir. Thank you." She bent down to take up her valise.

"William!" Her escort summoned a beautifully liveried footman standing near by. "See to madam's luggage. And we'll be off immediately." He turned to Louise. "Will you step into the carriage?" He presented his arm. Louise took it, her eyes cast down. She was biting her lower lip with mortification.

They were quickly settled against the soft leather cushions, sitting side by side, her escort staring stonily out the window opposite hers. After a brief delay during which her two trunks were loaded, the driver and the footman mounted the carriage, and with a smart snap of the whip they were off.

The drive was filled with exotic sounds,

sights, and smells. Louise was constantly on the point of exclaiming or pointing or questioning. But her silent and grim companion prevented her from giving free rein to her excitement. Then, like an evil fairy, the reason for her trip came back to her, and she started guiltily at feeling so vibrantly curious when she should be planning the best way of finding Charles as speedily as possible. She was on the point of requesting advice from her escort, but a glance in his direction showed her his saturnine profile staring at the passing scene and quelled the impulse.

They seemed to be traveling toward ever more magnificent surroundings. The houses were becoming larger and more ornate, the people on the streets were more exquisitely turned out, and the carriages were all as luxurious as the one she was riding in. Rather than finding this a comfort, Louise began to feel apprehensive at the meeting with her aunt, and could not help contrasting her own plain cotton frock with those creations she glimpsed on the backs of the occasional women they passed. Then the carriage stopped, and Louise looked up. She gasped.

They were in front of the grandest house she had ever seen.

"Where are we?" she asked timidly.

"Where are we?" he repeated coldly. "Why, we are *there*. We are where you wanted to come. Will you descend?" And he offered her his arm. Louise weakly took it and left the carriage.

As they mounted the steps, the massive double doors were thrown open by liveried servants wearing powdered wigs, and Louise and her companion passed into a splendid foyer. The floors were of alternating black and white marble squares, and the whole was dominated by a sweeping curved staircase. The doors closed behind Louise just as she saw a woman begin to descend the stairs, a lorgnette held to her eyes. She was quite old, though thin and straight, and she was superbly gowned in high-waisted crimson muslin with matching ribbons, and had rubies at her throat. It seemed to Louise that her cheeks were unnaturally bright; then she realized that she was heavily rouged.

"Ah, madame. I have fetched your niece. May I be excused now?" said the man.

"My niece?" the woman queried, a look of astonishment on her face. "Are you playing jokes on your aunt, Henry? Who is this child and where ever did you find her?" As she raised her lorgnette for inspection, her expression became haughty. Louise felt faint.

Chapter 2

The three of them stood staring at each other for what seemed like minutes, while the liveried servants gawked. The older woman was the first to break the spell. Still looking at Louise, though having lowered her lorgnette, she said:

"Well, Henry? Are you amusing yourself at my expense? What is the meaning of this?"

"Indeed, madame, I was under the impression that I had fetched your niece to you." He turned a hostile look toward Louise, and spoke severely. "—An impression this young person did nothing to dispel." Then, speaking to Louise coldly, he added, "Why did you not correct me, ma'am? Why did you come with me? Surely I gave you sufficient opportunity to disclose your identity?"

All the fatigue and anxiety of the last few hours seemed to swoop to Louise's head. She felt her cheeks flush scarlet with shame and anger. She had never been so rudely treated, and now she was placed, like a butterfly on a pin, under the scrutiny of the flamboyant old woman, the haughty dark man, and the be-wigged and curious servants.

"Sir, I was to be met at the coach by my aunt. When you announced that you had been sent to find me by my aunt—or at least, by *an* aunt—I assumed that I was in the proper hands. I came with you, even though you treated me with condescension and hauteur. I made a mistake, it is true, but then, sir, so did you. If you will be kind enough to allow me the use of your carriage I shall rectify *my* mistake immediately." She stood very straight. Her bosom heaved and her blue eyes, which seemed to grow darker, did not waver from his surprised gaze. He seemed at a momentary loss for words, though he retained his elegantly casual stance, his head arrogantly tilted.

It was the crimson lady who responded from the staircase:

"My dear, there's no question of your leaving immediately without some refreshment. There *has* been a mistake, but one I find delightful. You must humor me and my nephew, and take something with us." She descended and put her hand on Louise's arm. "Let us go into the drawing room and straighten out this puzzlement."

The unexpected kindness, following so swiftly on the heels of her anger, nearly breached Louise's defenses. It was the first pleasant expression that anyone had granted her for many hours, and she was afraid she would weep. With a barely murmured "Thank you, ma'am," she allowed herself to be led into an exquisite room off the foyer. The floors were gleaming parquet, partially covered by a Chinese-style carpet. There was crystal, and porcelain, and rich burnished woods, and the walls were adorned with delicately traced trees, flowers, and birds. Louise had never seen a room so lovely. She was propelled to a chair of gilt beech and sank gratefully into it. She felt as though she could go no farther.

"And now, my dear, tell me who you are and where you come from, and what brings you to London." The old woman spoke in a kindly and animated fashion, seating herself near Louise. Her nephew remained aloofly at a distance, though he seemed interested in what she had to say. She told them briefly that she was Louise Engleston from Twelve Elms, and that she had had to come to London hurriedly on a family matter. When she was finished the older woman expressed surprise that a girl so young should be sent off alone.

"There was no one else who could come,

ma'am," Louise said simply. "And I was to
have been met by my aunt. . . ."

"Well, that is delightful for us," the
woman said affably. "Isn't that right,
Henry? Isn't this an agreeable accident?"
Her nephew bowed, a slight smile on his lips
but not in his eyes.

The doors were opened and an array of servants entered with platters and trays. Louise
was struck with the opulence of the refresh-
ments, and compared them with the simple
bread and butter served with tea at Twelve
Elms. As she was choosing a currant cake
from a plate, she turned timidly to the
woman.

"May I ask whom I have the honor of addressing?"

"Oh! My dear! What savages you must
think us! I am Isabel, Duchess of Bledrough.
And this is my nephew, Henry Trevenaugh,
Duke of Wickenshire."

Louise, startled at the magnificence of the
company she found herself in, shyly stated
that she was very pleased to make their acquaintance. She felt ill at ease, however, and
was eager to escape. She reflected that she
would be happy to arrive at Mrs. Hartshord's
dwelling, no matter how indifferent her welcome might be.

After finishing tea, she stirred and suggested that if it was not too much trouble, she
would appreciate being taken to her aunt.

"I shall not hear of it!" said the duchess. "I shall not let you go traipsing around the town. I'll send a man to your aunt's house so that she may send someone to fetch you. You were very lucky this time to have fallen into the hands of a gentleman," and she nodded roguishly at Trevenaugh, who remained impassive, "but I could not rest easy if I were again to send you out into the town alone. It is full of ne'er-do-wells and footpads." She summoned a servant and quickly dispatched him to Mrs. Hartshord's house. Then she turned to Trevenaugh.

"My dear Henry, I almost forgot. You must forgive me. Your cousin Amelia is not coming to London after all—at least for a while. It seems her mama has found something more suitable—or at least more certain—for her, nearer home. Though she didn't write that in her letter, that is what I surmise. I received the letter in this morning's post and sent a man around to your house, but you had already left." Her eyes twinkled mischievously. "I am sorry to disappoint you. Anyway, I thank you for indulging an old woman." She turned to Louise with a smile. "And we have got a visitor—even for a brief stay—after all, have we not? How shall we entertain you while we wait?"

Before Louise could answer, Trevenaugh bowed to the duchess and said, "With your permission, ma'am, I shall take leave of you."

He was unsmiling, but not so stern as before. Once again, in spite of herself, Louise was struck by his splendid appearance and the elegance of his movement.

"Of course, and thank you again, dear boy," said the duchess.

He turned to Louise and bowed, saying nothing, then left.

The duchess looked brightly at Louise and laughed wickedly.

"I fear I have vexed him. But he is so solemn since he returned from the Colonies— or, I guess, we don't call them that anymore. America—I suppose we shall have to get used to it."

Louise was surprised at the familiarity with which the duchess spoke of her nephew to a stranger, but nevertheless she asked, "Was he there long, ma'am?"

"No. A little more than a year. I suppose that might seem long to you, young as you are. Not to me. He supposedly was there on the Crown's business. But it was no secret that he left London because of an affair of the heart. I suspect he would still be there if his brother had not died suddenly, and he had not inherited the title. Ah, well, I'm sure you do not wish to be bored by family gossip."

Far from being bored, Louise was intrigued, not only by the information but by the freedom with which it was given. She was accustomed to the reticence of the country people with whom she had spent her life, and about whom she did not know as much as she had just been told of the Duke of Wickenshire.

"Of course," continued the duchess, "since he returned and has the title, he is suddenly considered an extremely attractive *parti*—a success he does not wear well, I fear. My niece Amelia, for example, was longing to meet her cousin. Or rather, Amelia's mother was longing to effect the meeting. Henry was aware that he was being eyed as a prize and became hostile to the poor girl, even though he has never seen her. You might have noticed that he was almost discourteous to you?"

Louise blushingly acknowledged with a nod that she had indeed noticed.

The duchess chattered merrily on. "Yes. Well, he thought you were Amelia, of course, and set himself against you, even after you proved to be nothing of the sort. He is very rigid, I fear—all the Trevenaughs are, but they soften with age. But you, my dear, tell me about yourself. Have you a special friend?"

The duchess smiled knowingly and raised a naughty eyebrow. With her unnaturally red cheeks, crimson gown, and rubies, the effect was raffish. Louise was drawn to her but, at the same time, confused. She had never met anyone of this sort before—a duchess who painted herself and resided in the most exquisite room she had ever seen . . . who bedecked herself in crimson muslin and rubies when most women her age were encased in black bombazine . . . a woman who seemed to freely tell all the secrets of her nephew and then carelessly proceed to draw out any *she* might have.

"No, ma'am, I have no particular friends. We are very much alone at Twelve Elms. . . . My father is not well of late, so we do not live in circumstances that encourage visiting, I fear."

"Ah! But now you are in town, so all that's changed. You will be visiting a great deal, and with your looks, will be very sought after. I envy you the time that is before you."

The duchess's lighthearted assumption that she was to amuse herself in London brought before Louise more strongly than ever the reason for her trip. The sudden realization that she was sitting idly by when she should be seeking out Charles caused her expressive face to darken with anxiety.

"Whatever is the matter, child?" the duchess asked, alarmed. "Is something troubling you? Do you feel unwell?"

"Oh, no, ma'am. I just—I just—" She was spared from completing the thought by the discreet entrance of one of the bewigged servants. He leaned toward the duchess and spoke quietly in her ear.

"Well, now, here's a development! My dear, you are left without an aunt! Your aunt has gone to Bath!" And the duchess regarded her with interested surprise.

It was the final blow. All the frustrations, anger, fears, and hopelessness finally overwhelmed her control, and Louise gave way to tears.

"My dear, my dear! She has just gone to Bath for the waters, I'm told. There is no reason for such anguish."

"I pray you pardon me, ma'am. . . . I don't usually make such a display of myself. If I can but withdraw somewhere for a few moments, I should be most grateful."

"Of course, child. How selfish I've been to keep you with me. You should've had some time alone before now, after such a trip." She summoned a servant who, after whispered directions from the duchess, led Louise up the grand staircase to a delightfully airy chamber. In a few minutes a maid entered bearing a jug of hot water and an armful of spotless linen. Then Louise was left alone.

She felt without resources. There was no one she could turn to, and nothing that could help her. Yet, remembering her father's insistent plea, and feeling again her own apprehensions about Charles's long silence, she knew that something had to be done. It was impossible for her to return to Twelve Elms without Charles, or at least without news of him. It was equally impossible for her to remain in London alone, without companion or chaperone—not merely because it would be flouting the conventions, but also because she knew that she was incapable of coping alone. She needed guidance and help. She hadn't even the vaguest idea about where to look for Charles—there had been no communication with him since he had left Twelve Elms. Both she and her father had assumed that he had called on their aunt, but now that seemed unlikely. So she was left without a hint as to where in this vast conglomeration of people she could find him. As she bathed her face and straightened her clothes, her mind became more numb and incapable of functioning. It was in a state of almost stolid passivity that she descended the stairs and found her way back to the exquisite drawing room.

The duchess was still there.

"See! You only needed to have a little time to yourself to regain calmness," she said brightly as Louise entered. Then she looked at her more closely and pursed her lips.

"But I fear you have not been able to wash away all your distress. Am I not right, child?"

"Oh, ma'am, truly I do not know what to do," Louise began, and before she could think any further, she told the duchess the whole story—of her father's urgent plea, of Charles's long absence, and of her own feelings of inadequacy in the face of the duty imposed upon her.

The duchess listened with sympathetic cluckings and nods of her head, and little pats on her arm and moues of vexation. When the account was finished she brightened at once, took Louise's hand, and said:

"So, all this worry over a 'lost' brother. My dear, young men are always going awry in London—and they always turn up. Calm yourself. I shall have Henry make inquiries for us, and we shall be informed before sundown about Master Charles Engleston. In the meantime you must rest and dine with me here."

She bustled about, summoning another of the seemingly endless supply of servants. Louise tried to protest, then tried to thank her, but, finding both attempts ignored, allowed herself to be led once more to the airy chamber she had just left. She sank gratefully onto the huge bed that dominated one corner. Soon, as much to escape her situation as from fatigue, she fell into a deep sleep.

She was awakened by a light tap at the door and the silent entrance of a maid, bearing a lighted candle, who asked if she wanted for anything and told her that Her Grace would be pleased to receive her below if it was convenient. Louise freshened herself as best she could, tried to smoothe the wrinkles from her worn traveling dress, and pinched some color into her cheeks. She looked at herself in the huge full-length mirror in one corner of the room and decided that she would have appeared bedraggled under the best of circumstances, but that against the elegant surroundings in which she found herself she looked distinctly shabby. She sighed and descended the sweeping staircase.

The doors to the drawing room were opened by footmen and she entered, to find the duchess seated facing Henry Trevenaugh, who was standing looking at ease amidst the splendor of the room. He was dressed in white satin breeches and a deep blue tail coat with gold buttons. His linen, which covered his neck and cascaded down his chest in ruffles, was impeccable. He held white gloves carelessly in his left hand, as though he had just arrived and removed them. He had been speaking, but stopped in midsentence, or so it seemed, when Louise entered.

He turned to her and bowed.

"Your servant, ma'am," he murmured. Though it was not a warm greeting, and his demeanor was still aloof and even cold, there was no more of the hostility that had marked their first meeting. Louise was nonplussed at the change. She curtsied, blushing as she did, and turned to the duchess.

The duchess also had changed her attire, and was much more regal in a grey silk high-waisted dress, with several strands of pearls at her throat and a small pearl diadem on her head. By candlelight it seemed that she was not as highly painted as earlier.

"How fresh and delightful you look after your rest, my dear. Isn't she delightful, Henry? Only England can produce such complexions, and then only in the country! It's like having a little flask of sea air delivered to my drawing room to find you here."

Louise felt herself blushing, and managed to thank the duchess faintly. She dared not look at Trevenaugh who, she was sure, must be remarking each element of her shoddy appearance. She found a chair and settled back into it, trying to be inconspicuous.

"As I told you he would, Henry has been very successful in his mission," said the duchess. "He was just giving me a report when you entered. Now he can tell us both what he has learned."

"You've found Charles?" said Louise, moving forward in her chair and grasping the arms. "Oh, where is he, sir? I'm so grateful to you."

Trevenaugh looked disturbed.

"Your gratitude is premature, ma'am," he

said. "I have not yet laid eyes upon your brother, but have had news of him."

"Has anything happened to him? Has he come to harm?"

Trevenaugh's manner seemed so constrained that all Louise's misgivings attacked with renewed vigor.

"Harm?—No—that is, he is still alive, so far as I know. He has come to no *physical* harm."

"What can you mean, Henry? You're being very tiresome, surely. What news of Master Charles?" The duchess spoke with asperity and tapped her fan on the arm of her chair for emphasis.

"Indeed, ma'am, I am doing my best to bear news of some delicacy. I do not know how to proceed any differently." He spoke with exasperation. He seemed ill at ease, and this stance was so unlike him that it struck a chill of apprehension into Louise's heart.

"Please, sir, tell me what it is that has happened to Charles. Can I go to him?"

"It would not be advisable to do so at the moment, ma'am," he said, regaining his composure. "I shall do what I can to get a message to him, telling him that you are in London."

"But where *is* he?" demanded the duchess.

"Madam, he is with Cleo de Merivange."

There was a pause.

"Ah, I begin to understand," said the

duchess, and she looked at Louise with dismay. Trevenaugh also regarded her, his face impassive.

Louise had no idea what his intelligence meant, but it carried an aura of dread.

Chapter 3

After a constrained silence, Louise said, "I do not understand. Who is this lady? What business has Charles with her?"

Trevenaugh remained impassive, and the duchess became agitated.

"Cleo de Merivange is . . . is . . ." the duchess began, and then stopped. For the first time since Louise had met her she seemed to lack words.

Trevenaugh's voice, cold as steel, cut in.

"Cleo de Merivange is a Circe, ma'am. She turns men to swine, and makes them pay a high price for the privilege."

As the realization came to her what he was saying, Louise gasped. She had imagined Charles the victim of violence, of kidnapping or of a blow on the head. It had never occurred to her that he might have been a willing collaborator in his disappearance. She was torn between relief at hearing he was unharmed and dismay at learning he was pos-

sibly involved in an unsavory situation, the
exact nature of which she could not grasp.

The duchess turned to Trevenaugh.

"You are perhaps being too strong,
Henry," she chided.

"I assure you, ma'am," he said, "anything
I say can give only a pale hint of the truth."
He laughed, but without mirth.

"But Charles has no money. We are not
poor, perhaps, but he has not the resources for
supporting a . . . a . . ."

"A courtesan." Trevenaugh said. "And the
most expensive—as well as the most heartless—
in the realm."

"Then . . . I do not understand. Charles is
so young, and without means. . . ."

"It's very simple, ma'am. Cleo de
Merivange has been quite successful in . . .
her profession. She has the means to indulge
herself if she chooses. She has taken up your
brother in the same way other women might
buy a pet monkey or a little blackamoor—
simply as a toy for her amusement. She will
doubtless weary of him soon, and toss him
aside."

Louise reacted angrily to the scorn in Trevenaugh's voice. Then she reflected that
Charles had indeed behaved reprehensibly if
what she heard was true, and that he deserved
censure. But regardless of his involvement,
she had to go to him.

"Can you give me the address of this lady, if you please."

"Oh, my dear," said the duchess with a sigh, "how little you understand the world you are dealing with. Do you think you could come within a mile of your brother if you were to suddenly appear on her doorstep like a beggar? She has the power to keep him hidden from you for the rest of her life, if she so chooses, and to humiliate you while doing so."

"My aunt is right, ma'am. Cleo de Merivange is quite ruthless and very powerful. It would never do for you to go directly to your brother. She has servants, and highly placed friends. If you wish, I shall endeavor to get a message to him, but . . ." and he paused with a somber look.

"What is it, sir?" asked Louise.

"Simply this. Do not be surprised if your brother is in no mood to heed your message. Do not be surprised if he should find it convenient to ignore you."

Louise flushed. "Charles would never do that. Once he knows that I am in London, and am concerned about him, he will come to me immediately."

Trevenaugh smiled faintly, and turned from her with a shrug of his shoulders.

The duchess shook her head and said: "I fear that Henry knows whereof he speaks, my child. This woman has methods which we decent women can't begin to comprehend. It might be that your brother is sufficiently enslaved to ignore all family feeling, all other demands save that of . . . pleasure. It has happened before, and with more worldly men than your brother, I fear." The duchess met Trevenaugh's impassive gaze.

"But I cannot just sit by, knowing that Charles may be in need of my help. Also, I have been entreated to learn whether he has been able to perform the errand for my father. My father's health, indeed his very life, I fear, depends upon receiving this information as soon as possible."

"I shall do what I can, ma'am, to reach your brother, or at the very least to get a message to him. Then we shall see the lay of the land." Trevenaugh spoke in an indifferent voice, almost bored, as though he were performing a tedious duty. Gone were the sparks of sympathy Louise had thought she discerned beneath his elegant exterior. He was once more the haughty man she had first met. She was confused at the transformation.

"And while Henry is off on his mission," said the duchess, "we shall not waste time. You need to circulate in society, to see and be seen, so that your stay shall not be wasted away in idle waiting. Tonight we shall dine and retire early, but tomorrow we shall sally forth into the world."

"Oh, ma'am, I have not the temperament

and—perhaps more important—have not the clothes for an entry into society. If it will not be too much of a burden on you, I would be grateful if I might stay under your roof for a day or so until Charles comes to me and we can return to Twelve Elms."

"Nonsense. I find it distasteful that anyone should cower out of sight, but particularly you, my child. You will do me credit. It's been too long since I've been seen in society, and I shall be seen to very good advantage with a delightful child such as yourself in my charge."

"But ma'am," Louise faltered. She was embarrassed—all the more so because she was tempted at the prospect of a glimpse of the glittering world she had heard rumors about at Twelve Elms. Then she remembered her shabby three dresses in the trunks, and the worn and creased garment she was wearing, and her much-mended shawl, and realized that exposure in such attire was impossible. "You are so very kind, ma'am. But I have not the means to take advantage of your generous offer. I must decline and once more beg your indulgence to allow me to rest with you quietly for a day or so."

"Means? *I* have means. That is no difficulty," said the duchess. Then, seeing that Louise was becoming ill at ease, she softened her voice and took the young girl's hand. "My dear, I am not offering you charity, but am asking that you be kind enough to indulge an old woman's whim. It would give me so much pleasure to show you to society. I have grown bored. If I can see the world again through young, inexperienced eyes, my boredom will dissipate. I am making a very selfish request when I ask you to let me present you to the world."

Louise did not understand very well the nature of the duchess's invitation, but the sincerity with which it was given was unmistakable. Yet she hesitated. She was not sure just what the duchess's largesse would entail, but she knew that it would be on a scale she had never encountered before. She did not feel that she had enough to offer in return, and was loath to be beholden—it went against her upbringing.

Furthermore, she felt uneasy under the cold and, she was sure, critical scrutiny of Trevenaugh. He had not moved or in any way made his feelings apparent, but she was certain he disapproved of her and what his aunt was doing. Yet she was not in a position to leave. She had nowhere to go, and if she was to find Charles and learn of the disposition of his errand, she would do so only under the protection of the duchess.

"Your kindness overwhelms me, ma'am—" Louise began.

"Not the least bit," said the duchess peremptorily. "You've made me very happy.

We shall amuse ourselves mightily come to-morrow. What do you think of my plan, Henry? Is it not a good idea to present the child to society? Once she is seen at Carlton House all London will be talking of her, and doubtless word will come to her brother's ear that she is in town."

Trevenaugh inclined his head. "That's possible, ma'am," he said without expression, "and it might be that should I fail to get a message to the young man, gossip will do so more effectively." He did not look at Louise.

"You see," said the duchess, "we shall all be conspiring to return your brother to your side as soon as possible."

Louise smiled doubtfully, but thanked her once more for her kindness. Trevenaugh took his leave, bowing to his aunt and stating that he would call the following afternoon. He inclined his head to Louise and murmured simply that he was her servant. His departure was graceful and swift. Though Louise had felt his presence somewhat oppressive, she found that his absence created a nagging emptiness. She was confused at her feelings.

She dined simply, listening to the duchess's inexhaustible fund of chatter, and retired early to the chamber above, which was now called hers.

● ● ●

Louise awoke to street sounds and household
bustle—the duchess's army of servants were
extremely noisy in going about their business
of readying the magnificent house for another day. Louise rose and went to the window, pulled the drapes, and was astonished at
the activity that was taking place under the
dazzling blue sky: Tradesmen were arriving
and leaving, servants were polishing and
chatting, farmers were hawking their wares
from horse-drawn wagons and handcarts. She
was happy to note that the day promised to
be warm, so she would be able to dispense
with her cloak that was so worn and un-
sightly. There was a knock on her door and a
maid entered, carrying tea and a message
from the duchess. Her Grace would wait
upon madam below, and would it be convenient to meet her in half an hour's time in
order to visit the dressmakers? Louise sent
word that indeed she would be pleased to be
ready in half an hour.

When she descended, she found the duchess
in the drawing room, her cheeks brightly
rouged, wearing a watered-silk morning coat
in lavender, with a matching bonnet saucily
garnished with ostrich feathers dyed the
same hue. Louise was becoming accustomed
to her flamboyant hostess, and found this attire almost discreet. Her own simple green
cotton frock with a square neck was cut in
the old style and drawn in at the waist. Her

bonnet was the same she had worn the day before, and she had a tan shawl thrown over her shoulders. She was struck by the discrepancy of their appearance, but the duchess immediately began to chat away about the plans for the day, and her lack of confidence diminished.

"My dear, how fresh you are. You have rested well? I hope so, for we have a *very* grueling day ahead of us. I have already sent word to Madame Lucille to expect us for fittings, and then we must go to my glovemakers, and search out some decent bonnets on Bond Street—and that is only the beginning. We must hurry, for I want you well rested for tonight, when we shall be going to Carlton House and you must look as fresh as you do now. . . . So we shall be off."

They left in a flurry of orders and commands that the duchess tossed at her staff of servants.

Madame Lucille's establishment was just off Bond Street, and was unprepossessing enough in appearance to reassure Louise. But once they were inside she felt as though she had been let into Aladdin's cave—there were bolts and bolts of satins, silks, organdies, in every imaginable color and weight. There were ribbons and feathers and buttons and spangles, and the whole scene was dominated by Madame Lucille, dressed in a severe and simple black frock of elegant lines.

"*Ah, c'est Madame la Duchesse*," she said when she saw them enter. "*Mais je vien de recevoir votre mot . . . vous me faite* great pleasure to come to my establishment. You are *belle* as always. And this is your ward? *Mais elle est ravissante!* What a joy to create beautiful dresses for her it will be!" Louise felt herself blushing and Madame Lucille clapped her hands to summon several seamstresses who set about measuring, while another group began to show the various cloths and ribbons, holding them next to Louise and regarding the duchess for approval.

"The blue!" said the duchess. "Definitely the blue to bring out the eyes. And the white muslin, of course, for one of the ball gowns . . . and the turquoise ribbons . . . and yes, I think the green *peau de soie*. . . . No, not the yellow, it makes her look sallow . . . absolutely, we must have the rose silk. . . ." And so on until Louise became stupified with the parade of colors and textures. She had assumed that they would be purchasing two or at the most three gowns—she had not envisioned this wholesale attack on Madame Lucille's wares. She was beginning to feel more and more strange, yet dared say nothing about it to the duchess in front of the volatile Frenchwoman and her army of seamstresses.

After three hours of being jabbed, measured, and manipulated, Louise was too exhausted to protest. As it seemed they were finishing, the duchess said:

"And have you something the child can wear now? She needs her spirits lifted, and a new frock on her back will do the job nicely, I believe."

"Ah, but yes! It happens that I have a dress ordered for the daughter of the Lady Ayreshore—she who has just eloped, perhaps madame has heard? Yes? *C'est une scandale, non?* But she was the same figure as mademoiselle, though not nearly so *belle*. Perhaps with just a little adjustment . . ."

The dress was brought. It was a filmy *eau de nil* muslin, and the most exquisite garment Louise had ever seen. During the long fitting and parade of materials, she had not bothered imagining the final results. Now, held tantalizingly before her, was a finished dress, ready to be worn. She was helped into it, and immediately felt its richness.

"Yes," said the duchess, "I knew I was right. All you needed to become one of the town Incomparables was a little artifice. Madame Lucille, send to one of the shops for some lotions—the child's face looks naked— and can you manage to find a bonnet and shawl to complement your creation?. . . . Quickly! We must be on our way. We have a thousand things to do and the morning has sped by."

Shopwomen were dispatched, and returned

with a selection. Louise's face was salved and powdered, and her lips were delicately tinted. She had always considered "painting" to be unsuitable for ladies, if not absolutely wicked, but whatever defenses she had were overridden by the duchess's high-handed commands. A bonnet was chosen and placed on her head, and a feather-light wool shawl, as delicately colored as an apple blossom, was placed on her shoulders.

Madame Lucille and her assistants stood to one side regarding her, and the duchess sat before her, looking very pleased.

"Is it . . . suitable, ma'am?" Louise asked, feeling shy under such scrutiny.

"Suitable? Madame Lucille, lead the child to the big mirror in the back. Let her judge whether it is 'suitable.' "

Louise was led to the mirror and stopped, startled at the creature she saw. The eyes were brighter, the skin more glowing, the figure more elegant than any she had ever seen. A wand had been waved and she had been transformed. She had become beautiful.

She looked away, fearing to be thought vain if she gazed too long at the image of her changed self. The duchess nodded happily and turned to Madame Lucille.

"Very well done. Now you must deliver all these dresses at once. No later than tonight."

"*Mais, c'est impossible!*" objected Madame Lucille, her eyes widened in shock. "Maybe

I can have one dress for tonight—at the most two—but the rest will take another two days at the least, and that with my ladies working all night as well as all the day."

"Two then, this evening," said the duchess. "And early in the evening, mind you. We shall need the white one for Carlton House. Come child, we must be off on the remainder of our task. We have to find bonnets and gloves and shoes. . . . Well, no point in talking—let's be doing." She gathered her fan and reticule and led the way to the waiting carriage.

Louise followed in a daze. She had entered the shop a shabby provincial, and she left it a glowing beauty—it seemed she was even moving differently. She could not help noticing that the footman who handed her into the carriage did so with more deference than he had summoned to help her out when she had arrived.

The rest of the day was a whirl of shops, tradespeople, scents, and textures. There was swansdown, the Spanish leather, kid and velvet, essence of rose, ribbons from Lyons, ostrich feathers, and fans from China. The assault on Louise's senses was unlike anything she had ever experienced before. She was, at the end of the afternoon, exhausted—not so much physically, but by the incredible variety of sensations that had been presented her.

The duchess, on the other hand, seemed

fresher than when she had left that morning. She was indefatigable, demanding ever more finery and searching out ever more exquisite artifices. She blithely commandeered a shop when she entered, quickly reduced its contents to a pile at her feet, and imperiously chose the objects she needed, before setting out to the next place. She was blooming by the end of the afternoon, when she noticed that Louise was beginning to droop.

"My dear! We must get you home and get you rested for tonight. You are pale with exhaustion. As usual, I've been selfish and unthinking."

"Quite the contrary, ma'am, you have been generosity personified. I don't know how I can ever repay your kindness. Indeed, I am at a loss to even begin to thank you properly—"

"We'll talk no more about it," said the duchess with a wave of her fan. "There are not many pleasures left me now, but one of the supreme pleasures I have is acquiring things—even if for other people. The act of acquisition, for me, is an end in itself and an extremely agreeable one.

Louise was a little shocked at the disclosure—running so counter to her thrifty upbringing at Twelve Elms. Since, however, she was the recipient of the duchess's current bent for acquisition, she could not readily arrive at an appropriate attitude, so she put the matter out of her mind. She settled back in the carriage as they rode to the duchess's residence, and tried to remember that at this time the day before she had been on a lumbering coach in disagreeable company, wending her way toward London. It was as though she had been another person.

They arrived and descended.

"Ah," said the duchess, gesturing toward another carriage that was waiting in front of the house. "I see Henry is here. Perhaps he has news for us, my dear."

Louise felt a chill pass over her as she was reminded of the reason for her being here. The activities of the morning had all but erased what had been her overriding concern when she had arrived. Now, with a start of guilt, heightened because she had taken so much pleasure in the last few hours, she thought of Charles and wondered whether he was waiting above with the duke.

Hastily they ascended the steps and entered the house.

Chapter 4

As she lifted her arms to pamper her golden curls into order, her peignoir slipped open and Charles caught a glimpse of her breast. He thought, with a pang, that it was the whitest, softest, and most desirable object he had ever seen. She saw his face reflected in the mirror, saw his transfixed gaze, and, with a smile, closed the garment at her throat.

"Charlie, my dove, would you please pull the cord? I fear I shall have to get Effie to fix my hair. It seems to be rebelling."

He became surly at the instant, but did as he was told. He had hoped to spend time alone with Cleo, without the ever-present servants and maids with whom she surrounded herself. Of late, it seemed, they were never alone. There were always either visitors or tradesmen or the inexhaustible supply of servants parading in and out of Cleo's boudoir. Her boudoir was, in fact, one of the most public places he had ever been.

It had not been like that at the beginning. They had spent intoxicating days alone, when they had first met. Their first hours together, from the time he had been summoned from the street to the woman in the closed carriage, through their first tentative, then passionate exchanges in this very room, had been the most ecstatic that Charles had ever known. He thought back on them with a mixture of regret and desire.

He tugged the cord roughly and turned back to Cleo.

She was watching him, her green eyes narrowed speculatively and a hint of a smile hovering around her mouth.

"You seem restless, my pet. Perhaps you need exercise? A ride in the park would do you some good. I'll have a horse saddled for you, shall I?"

"No!" he said vehemently, causing her eyes to narrow even more with displeasure. He perceived his mistake, and softened his voice. "No, Cleo. Don't send me away again. I'm not restless, and have done nothing but ride these last few days. In fact I've almost exhausted your stable, since I have been forbidden to come near you."

"Forbidden?" she said softly, laughing. "That's much too strong a word, my little precious. Forbidden, indeed. I was not well, and needed some time alone, some time to myself. Surely you wouldn't begrudge me that?"

He turned miserably from her. "You were not ill. I saw you riding in your carriage. You never . . . never . . . looked . . . more beautiful. . . . Yet when I came here I was told you could not receive me. You have been lying to me."

"And my little Charlie has been spying," she said harshly, her long fingers drumming lightly on the vanity table in front of which she was sitting.

He was alarmed. "No, I was not spying, Cleo. I saw you by accident." His blue eyes were full of pleading and his black hair fell over his forehead in a mass of glistening curls which highlighted his tanned complexion. She was stirred again by his young masculine appeal and turned toward him, just as the knock came on the door.

With a shrug and a tantalizing smile, she gave the permission to enter. Charles stifled the words that leapt to his mind. He settled miserably in a *bergère* while the buxom young maid fussed with Cleo's hair.

"And what are you planning today, Charlie?" Cleo asked while carefully scrutinizing herself in the mirror.

He gave a bitter laugh. "Why, whatever you would have me do," he said, and stared sullenly at his feet, which were stretched before him. Cleo regarded him in the mirror.

"You *are* restive. You need some occupation, something to keep your mind busy—you should take up cards. Not only would it soothe you, it would possibly help to augment your fortune."

"My fortune!" he said with a snort of disgust. "You know I have no fortune—the only money I had has long since disappeared,—" He looked as though he would say more, but his eyes met hers in the mirror. His were the first to disengage the stare and fall again to his boots.

"I do not remember having used coercion to part you from those few pounds," she said with a smile. "And, furthermore, I have spent more than that sum on clothing, feeding, and amusing you these last few months. You have, I believe, gotten the better part of the bargain."

He was crimson with shame to be spoken to in this manner, particularly in front of a servant—who, however, appeared to notice nothing amiss and seemed not even to hear what was being said as she enticed Cleo's hair into a crown of golden ringlets. His eyes flashed to Cleo's in the mirror. She regarded him coolly, with a smile on her lips.

"So, Charlie, let us hear no more about your lost resources. You used the money to buy me a pretty little bracelet—I shall cherish it always, my pet—but your investment has paid you very well. How true it is, what they say about casting bread upon the waters." She laughed, throwing her head back and exposing a row of small, very white teeth between her tinted lips. Even in this moment of hating he could not help but desire her.

He clenched his fists and was silent for a long moment. When he spoke it was with restraint. "You mock me, Cleo. Perhaps you have always done so. But I have always, from the very first, had only respect and love for you. The 'little bracelet' I bought you with money that had been entrusted to me to perform a duty, a grave duty, and I have betrayed the trust for you. It evidently seemed paltry to you. It was all, everything I had to give, and I lay it at your feet."

She was touched by his speech, and possibly would have gone to him if the maid had not been present. After the first wave of sentiment receded, however, reason regained control, preventing her from reciprocating with some foolish and expensive gesture, such as offering to return the bracelet.

"My precious, do you think that I don't appreciate your gift? It is very dear to me—as are you. I was not aware of this betrayed trust. Do you owe money to someone?"

"Let us speak no more about it. I lost control of my reason . . . I had not intended to talk of it to you." Charles was mollified by the softness in her voice.

"But we must speak about it. You must

have no secrets from me. Tell me, my pet, to whom do you owe money?"

Charles hesitated, then all restraint was swept away by her sympathy.

"It is not I who owe money. I was given that money by my father to bring to London to put in the hands of a certain man. I was to have done so over two months ago. I don't know why my father is sending this man money, but I do know he set great store upon his having it. That is the trust I betrayed."

Cleo was touched. This was not the first time, certainly, that someone had risked ruin for her, but it was a gesture that never failed to thrill her. It gave her a control over lives that was almost as essential to her well-being as money. And she was attracted to Charles. Now she took his head lightly in her hands and held it as though she were appraising a new jewel, admiring once more his classically sculpted features infused with the vivid colors of youth and health.

"My little pet, we shall take care that you do not face ruin. The sum you spent was large, certainly, by your standards, but it was not a king's ransom. It can be recouped if you're willing. A friend of mine can be very helpful in this matter, someone we shall be meeting later tonight, perhaps, at Josie's party. I shall talk to him, possibly introduce you, and we shall see what can be done."

Charles was newly humiliated to be so patronized by Cleo, and he jerked his head from her light grasp and turned away.

"I do not require your help," he said stiffly.

"Oh, but you do, my pet." Cleo laughed and moved back to the vanity table. "Or rather, you need the help I can get you from Lord Castleton—"

She stopped in midsentence when she saw the reaction the name caused. Charles looked at her with startled eyes and grew pale. His stare became hostile and his nostrils flared. For a moment neither said anything; then Cleo dismissed the maid. She turned to Charles.

"Well, and what's this all about? Do you know Lord Castleton?"

"You are a devil," he said in a low, wondering voice. "You are mocking me."

"My dear Charlie, you presume too much. What is this talk of devilment and mockery? You confuse me." Cleo spoke lightly, but she was intrigued and was determined to learn the significance of Charles's behavior. He was agitated and was looking at her with accusing eyes.

"You have known from the beginning, and have been sporting with me."

"Known *what*, Charlie?" Cleo was becoming annoyed. She hated mystification, and it struck her that Charles was acting like a naughty child who would not divulge his latest mischief. She spoke sharply. "Enough of this nonsense. Either tell me what it is that you are talking about or take your leave. I am not in the mood to indulge you."

The threat of expulsion had its effect. The accusation faded from Charles's eyes, to be replaced with pleading.

"Forgive me, Cleo. I . . . I have been so distraught. And when you mentioned Lord Castleton . . . I could not understand why his name should be known to you, unless it was because you were aware of my business with him. I have been so tightly strung of late . . . what with the disposition of the money and not being able to see you. I have given over to unhealthy imaginings. . . . Forgive me."

"Poor Charlie. Of course I forgive you." Once more she was drawn to him, knowing that he was again totally in her power, and would deliver to her anything she might demand. "Now, what is this secret about Castleton? From where do you know him?"

"I do not know him. I have never laid eyes on him." Charles spoke reluctantly, turning from her. "I could not even tell you what he looks like."

"I have no need of you to tell me what he looks like," said Cleo with sharpness, mingled with amusement. "I know that—and in greater detail, I daresay—better than most people. What is your business with him?"

"It was to Lord Castleton that I was to deliver the sum of money that I spent . . . spent for the bracelet that I gave you." He lowered his voice with shame.

She was surprised. "Whatever for? Why would you bring such a sum to Castleton?"

"I don't know," said Charles, his voice lower and his gaze averted. "It was not my affair. It was a commission for my father."

"But surely you have some idea as to why your father would want to send Castleton money?"

"No. None."

"But that's extraordinary. Castleton is very rich, my pet. The sum of money over which you are so concerned is of no significance to him. He has lost that much and more at cards in an hour's time and walked away from the table smiling."

Charles flushed. "It is not a paltry sum to me or my father. I was astounded to learn he had so much at his command."

"Oh, Charlie, I am not trying to belittle you. I was merely making an observation." She stroked his hair and caressed his face, but looked speculatively into space. After a few minutes she asked, "Is this the first time your father has sent such a sum to Castleton?"

"I don't know. I know nothing of his affairs. He is very close. . . . Only, every year, for almost as long as I can remember, he has made a trip to London each spring, and returned from it in a most unhappy state of mind. What his business was, I cannot say."

"This is very interesting, pet. It now seems to me imperative that you meet with Castleton. I'm sure he will be curious to see you." She spoke lightly.

"Do not toy with me, Cleo," Charles said, angrily withdrawing his head from her hands.

"You are too sensitive, Charlie. I am trying to get to the bottom of this, and to help you. Now control yourself. Was Castleton expecting you?"

"I don't know. I think not. My father had planned to come himself, as usual, until the last minute, when he felt too ill to undertake the trip. I suppose he felt it was not necessary to send word, since I was to have arrived, performed my commission, and returned straightaway. . . ." He kept his eyes averted and his head inclined.

"But you were . . . detained," she said with a laugh, and reached for him again. He stiffened momentarily, then became pliant in her hands. "And happily for me, my precious." She spoke sincerely. Now that he was suddenly enveloped in mystery, his value for her was enhanced. She felt a renewed interest in him. "So we must set about getting this affair in order. I believe that Castleton will be at Josie's reception this evening. I will take you with me and we shall meet him there."

"I cannot meet him without the money—I would be humiliated."

"Oh, Charlie, I'm offering you help. Don't be foolish enough to refuse it. Talk to Castleton. Let us learn what's at the bottom of all this."

"You find this an amusing conundrum," he said moodily. "But it's my honor that is in question."

"Well, the sooner the matter is cleared up the sooner your honor will be restored. There's no point in skulking when help is at hand. And I can help you, Charlie, for I know Castleton very well." She smiled at him with her eyes half closed. "You must let me do what I can for you, my pet. Let me use the influence I have. There will be no dishonor attached to my efforts. On the contrary, that's the way business is conducted in town."

What Cleo was offering was repugnant to Charles; it went counter to his upbringing to let a woman interfere in business, in an affair of honor. But a great deal of his behavior for the last few months had been against his upbringing, so he had no defenses left.

"Very well. I shall go with you to your party tonight."

"Come, come, pet. Let's be a little more

sprightly in our acceptance. After all, it is a party, not an execution." She tweaked his nose.

He twisted his head away from her, but she persisted, and shortly they were both laughing together as they touched and teased each other. Whatever scruples Charles had, they evaporated, and he was willing to do anything Cleo wished of him.

As their game was becoming less childlike and more adult in its urgency, there was a knock at the door. With a sigh of exasperation Charles tried to keep Cleo from answering by holding his hand over her mouth. Laughing, she broke away from him.

"It might be important, Charlie," she whispered, arranging her peignoir. "Come in," she called.

The maid entered and curtsied.

"Mr. Brombedge is below to see you, ma'am," she said.

"Aha," said Cleo, with interest. "Show him up."

"Why must you see him now? Can't he wait?"

"My pet, this is very fortunate. Brombedge is Castleton's secretary. Obviously Castleton wishes to . . . discuss something with me. Your introduction shall be much easier than I thought."

"What would he want to discuss?" asked Charles, instantly jealous, his eyes somber.

"This is a business matter, pet, and none of your concern. Hello, Brombedge," she said, as a very thin man dressed in a black, elegantly cut coat entered the room. His sparse hair was dyed as black as his coat, framing his gaunt white face. His eyes were deep set, and black also, and sparkled with an unnatural and feverish brightness. His thin lips were as colorless as the rest of his face, and were set firmly, as though they covered clenched teeth. He bowed.

"Your servant, ma'am," he said with deference, in a soft, self-effacing voice.

"What have you brought me?" Cleo asked peremptorily.

"This note, ma'am, from his lordship. He begged that you return an answer with me."

Cleo broke the seal and read the note hastily, then pursed her lips and read it again more slowly.

"Tell his lordship that I shall be at Josie van Scuyden's reception tonight, and we can discuss this matter further there, if he wishes." She folded the note and placed it in a box on her vanity.

"His lordship asked specifically that you return his note and send him a written answer, ma'am. If it wouldn't be too much trouble—"

"But it would be too much trouble, Brombedge," said Cleo with a sarcastic smile. "I have no intention of sending his lordship a written note. And I shall keep his note as a reminder that I am to have the pleasure of seeing him later this evening."

"If you please, ma'am—"

"That will be all, Brombedge." And she turned her back on him. His manner had not altered during their exchange, though his eyes had become more opaque and with-drawn.

"Very well, ma'am," he said, bowing to both Cleo and Charles, swiftly scrutinizing the latter as though to record him in his memory. He silently slipped from the room.

"Who is that man, Cleo, and what business can you have with him?" Charles had been chilled by the fast regard that Brombedge had thrown him, and the whole encounter had left him feeling uneasy.

"These are grown-up matters, pet. Don't concern yourself with them," said Cleo with a distracted wave of her hand. She moved toward Charles as though to continue their interrupted game. But he had been stung by her reply, and stood rigid with barely con-tained fury.

"Do not treat me this way, Cleo, do not dismiss me as though I were a lackey. Do you scorn me that you can wave me away like a troublesome insect?" For an instant it seemed that he might strike her, and her eyes narrowed guardedly.

"If you are not happy here, Charlie, you

have always my permission to leave," she said coldly. She watched him gain control of himself and turn from her, with passion fighting pride on his face.

"You know I have no wish to leave you," he said after a long pause. Gradually he unclenched his fists and let her lead him where she would.

Chapter 5

When they arrived at the house and the duchess pointed out Trevenaugh's carriage, Louise's first thought had been that he would surely have news of her brother. As she hastily ascended the steps to the entrance she briefly wondered whether Trevenaugh would notice her changed appearance, and, if so, whether he would approve. Then she was annoyed with herself for having entertained such an idea, when so many others should have been occupying her mind. The double doors of the entrance were swung open, and the duchess swept into the foyer, followed by Louise. They went directly to the drawing room, where Trevenaugh was awaiting them.

"What news?" said the duchess, rushing into the room and discarding her fan, reticule, day coat, and bonnet as she went. "What have you found, Henry?"

"Good afternoon, ma'am," said Henry ironically, with a bow. "I have little enough news, though what I—" He caught sight of Louise, who had followed more demurely in the duchess's flamboyant wake. He seemed momentarily surprised, and looked at her for a few seconds as though he were trying to recall who she was. He quickly regained control of himself, and continued, "—what I have is important enough. I have found where the young man lodges. It has not been with Cleo de Merivange, though he seems to be in very little of the time. I have left a message with his porter, asking him to call on you at his earliest convenience."

"Then I shall probably see him today," said Louise.

"That is not at all certain, ma'am," Trevenaugh said, turning to her with a cautiously admiring look. He spoke with less of his customary hauteur. "It appears that your brother is away a good deal of the time, and for very long periods. It is not likely that he will get my message today." He continued to regard her, after he had finished speaking. Louise felt embarrassed.

"No matter," said the duchess, "he would be an encumbrance today, since we are going to Carlton House this evening." She settled into one of the gilt beech chairs. "You are going with us, of course, Henry?"

"Of course, ma'am," Trevenaugh said with a slight smile.

Without a pause the duchess said, "And

what do you think of our visitor? I should hardly have recognized her myself. Isn't she a beauty? It takes but a very little art to act as a foil for natural beauty—but that little bit is essential."

"Indeed, ma'am, I understand now what is meant by gilding a lily."

Louise had been recovering from the effects of Trevenaugh's initial scrutiny when the duchess spoke, but now the renewed interest in her appearance from both of them, and the compliment from Trevenaugh, wrecked her composure. She blushed furiously, and the more she blushed the more embarrassed she became. She was not accustomed to compliments on her appearance, and had grown up thinking she was sound and reasonably well favored, nothing more. To suddenly be the object of admiration left her feeling exposed.

"Look at the child blush," crowed the duchess. "You must get accustomed to receiving favorable notice, my child. You may blush if you must—but in moderation, only. Otherwise the effect is spoiled."

Louise was spared from making a reply by the entrance of the servants with tea. She remained quiet and as unobtrusive as possible during the refreshment. At the end of it she was calm again, and was able to glance at Trevenaugh without any visible reaction as she bid him good day. He promised to call for them later that evening in order to escort them to Carlton House, and Louise retired to her room for some much-needed rest.

She fell into a deep sleep almost as soon as she had touched the bed. She was awakened by a tapping at her door and the entrance of a maid with several large white boxes trimmed in gilt. She was momentarily confused, then she realized that these were the first of the dresses that Madame Lucille had promised to finish for that evening. She watched with fascination as the maid unpacked a white muslin ball gown with turquoise ribbons and held it up for her inspection.

"It's very pretty, ma'am, and your ladyship will look very pretty in it, I'm sure," the little girl said, bobbing and fussing with the other package, which contained the rose silk morning dress. Louise was nonplussed to be called a "ladyship," and started to correct the maid, when another knock was followed by the impetuous entry of the duchess.

"They've arrived, I see. Madame Lucille kept her promise. She'd better. They're lovely, my dear. Quickly, let's try them to see if they fit. The muslin first, for that's what you'll be wearing this evening. Everyone will be there—the *bon ton en masse*. If ever there were a time to be seen to one's best advantage, this is it."

"We're going to Carlton House, ma'am? You are speaking of the *Prince's* residence?"

Louise had not really comprehended that she was to be calling on royalty before now. Suddenly she was awed by the prospect.

"The Prince *Regent's* residence, my dear. Yes, that's where we're going. Though it were no great matter if that's *all* we were going to do—simply go to see *him*. But, fortunate child that you are, you have arrived just at the right time, for tonight the Prince Regent is giving a ball that has been the talk of the whole town for the last few weeks. *Everyone* will be there—from two continents, for His Highness is entertaining the Bourbons, so recently exiled by that French dwarf who's making such a nuisance of himself. And that is why you must look your best."

Louise reflected that in such a grand assemblage it seemed unlikely that she would be singled out for attention. She tried on the dresses with interest, nevertheless, and was again delighted at what she saw in the mirror. After the dresses had been judged satisfactory, the duchess gave orders to the maid to start the preparation of the baths for herself and Louise. They were to be at Carlton House for dinner, which just gave them time for a leisurely *toilette*.

During the next two hours Louise was pampered in steaming water carried by the pailful from below, and scented with fragrances she had never suspected existed. Her black hair was brushed until it gleamed, and then was carefully dressed in such a way as to suggest she had just casually tossed the curls into place. She was salved, rubbed with lotions, and her face artfully tinted. The white muslin was slipped over her head. It fitted to perfection. The waist was very high—just below the breasts, in the new style—and the bodice was cut very low, exposing more of her bosom than she thought seemly. She timidly enquired of the maid if she thought a fichu would be in order. The maid thought not, but promised to relay the request to Her Grace. Other than, perhaps, offering too much exposure, the dress was more lovely than she could have dreamed. It fell in cloudlike folds to just below her ankles, and was trimmed at the bodice with two flowing turquoise ribbons that enhanced the blue of her eyes. As she was dressing, she could not help but wonder that she was preparing to go to a ball given by the Prince Regent. Such a thing would have been unthinkable two days before, and now she was treating the situation almost as though it were a commonplace. She had marveled that she should be allowed at such short notice to participate in so exclusive an occasion, and had asked the duchess why this was. The duchess had appeared astonished at the question.

"Why, because you are with *me*, child,"

she had replied, and had proceeded to talk of other things.

A maid announced that the Duke of Wickenshire was below, and waited the pleasure of her company. Louise felt more confident than she could ever remember feeling. She was disturbed at the low cut of the gown, but she decided that it was not something to reflect on her, and could easily be corrected by the addition of a fichu if the duchess deemed it necessary.

She descended the staircase with poise and glided past the footman who opened the door to the drawing room. The duchess was there with Trevenaugh, and both turned to stare at her as she entered. For a long moment neither spoke. Then the duchess simply said, in a soft admiring voice:

"Oh, my dear."

Louise was determined not to blush like the country girl she was every time an approving glance was thrown her way. But the regards of both were so openly appreciative that she could not control the flush she felt spreading across her face.

The duchess seemed not to notice, however, for after a pause she continued, "And what's all this talk of a fichu? I think you might with advantage wear my pearls, but certainly not a fichu. . . . What do you think, Henry?"

"A fichu would be criminal, ma'am, and

even pearls would be a desecration," he said. There was irony in his smile, certainly, but there was another quality in both smile and voice that Louise had not met with before— an undercurrent of feeling that both pleased and disturbed her.

"You are both very kind," she said, and to preclude any further discussion of herself she turned to the duchess. "You, ma'am, are very beautiful."

The duchess was certainly splendid in lavender and white satin, blazing with diamonds and amethysts in a necklace at her throat and a tiara on her head. Trevenaugh was more sober, though equally impressive, in a black velvet tail coat, white satin knee breeches, and blindingly white linen. His color was high, as though he had been riding, and Louise regarded him with discreet admiration.

"Thank you, my dear," said the duchess, pleased. "Indeed, the three of us are a notable contribution to the ball. I hope His Highness appreciates us fully. Now we should go there in order to give him the opportunity to do so." She summoned the coach and in a few minutes they were on their way.

They rode to Carlton House in a closed carriage, chatting easily but with the restrained excitement that seizes people just before an event. As they approached the royal residence they fell into line with other carriages, and their pace slowed to a processional trot, until finally they arrived at the entrance. The doors were opened and they were helped to the steps.

They proceeded to the garden. It was with an effort that Louise managed to keep her mouth from dropping open, for they had stepped into a magic world. Every tree and shrub was festooned with jewellike lanterns that glimmered against the darkness and cast a glow over the setting. There seemed to be soft music everywhere, yet there were no musicians visible (they had been hidden by banks of orchids) and in the center of the garden was a huge statue of a swan that seemed to be made of crystal, but on closer inspection proved to be of ice. It was revolving slowly, inexplicably, coruscating from the shimmering multicolored lanterns. Tables were set about everywhere, covered with flowers and silver and attended by servants in the royal livery. The air was perfumed with myriad blossoms. All the people seemed to be endowed with beauty. It was an atmosphere that surpassed fantasy.

Louise was so enchanted that she forgot for a few moments the existence of her companions. The duchess broke the spell.

"Very nicely done," she said appraisingly, "though excessive in some of the details."

"Oh, ma'am," said Louise, "I have never seen anything so lovely."

"No, my child, I daresay you haven't. But you are very young. I suppose this is a scene I should like to see with young eyes. Oh, well, we must get to our table and be in place before His Highness arrives."

"Are we to dine here?" asked Louise in wonderment.

"Certainly not," said the duchess. "Or rather, some people will dine here, but *we* shall be in the conservatory at His Highness's table."

Louise had been so startled by so many events in the last two days that her capacity for surprise was diminished. She accepted the announcement matter-of-factly.

The conservatory at Carlton House had been built in the Gothic style, with high vaulted ceiling and stone pillars. It looked rather like a nave in a cathedral. It had been transformed for the occasion, with flowers placed on every available surface, and was glowing from hundreds of candles. A table had been set down the center, long enough to seat three hundred people, and it was covered with flowers and silver baskets of grapes, peaches, pineapple, apricots—in short, every fruit Louise had ever imagined. The setting was dominated by a huge silver basin at the head of the table, placed before the Prince Regent's chair, from which two streams meandered down each side of the table, channeled in silver troughs. In the streams were swimming gold and silver fish.

Surrounding the table were a group of glitering and, to Louise's eye, very formidable people. She gradually felt more at ease, however, as the duchess, who was treated with deference by anyone she chose to acknowledge, brought her to the notice of various acquaintances. Louise, as an appendage to the duchess, was accorded the same consideration. Trevenaugh, too, seemed to be highly regarded, though he was approached cautiously and without much warmth. Louise noticed that he mostly remained aloof from conversation once he had performed a perfunctory greeting. His expression, though not hostile, was far from affable.

There was a sudden hush in the room, similar to the silence that falls in the forest when a dangerous animal is in the vicinity. This silence was more benign, however, for it signaled the entry of George, Prince Regent of England, who was ceremoniously wending his way through his guests. He was upon Louise before she was aware of the significance of the sudden change of manner about her.

A heavy, rather short man with a florid face and a most gorgeous uniform stopped in front of the duchess.

"Well, well, 'pon my soul, I do believe

this is Isabel, Dowager Duchess of Bledrough. It is a long time, madame, since we have had the pleasure. I hope we shall not have to wait another long period to feast our eyes on you."

"Your Highness is too kind," said the duchess with unwonted demureness, and made a low and very elegant curtsy. "And may I introduce my young friend, Miss Louise Engleston, who is visiting me."

Louise had not expected this, but she hastily curtsied, keeping her eyes cast down.

He gave her his hand and guided her to a standing position, regarding her all the while with open admiration.

"Indeed, madame, if you bring friends like this with you I shall insist you make daily visits." He smiled at Louise. "I hope we shall be seeing you often during the season, ma'am."

Not knowing what to say, Louise curtsied again as he left her to proceed around the room, followed by a tall, Junoesque, rather chilling woman who was, she learned later, his particular friend, Lady Hertford.

Suddenly Louise found herself the center of attention. Everyone was pressing near her, seeking introductions and flattering and flirting. Some of the women unveiled their animosity toward one of their own who had been complimented by royalty. If she had had time to think she would have been undone by all the notice she was receiving. But the onslaught was so quick and the force so overwhelming that she was taken by surprise. She had to rely on her instincts, which were sound, so that her responses to all the overtures, both friendly and hostile, were models of decorum and charm. She tasted for the first time in her life the heady pleasure of winning admiration. The delicate flush that heightened Louise's color now was not the blush of an embarrassed young woman, but the sign of high spirits. Her demeanor remained calm but her eyes sparkled and her gestures lost their constraint.

Though her conversation was not noticeably witty, and she was incapable of returning the badinage of some of her more sophisticated admirers, her manner was so direct and forthright that it was found to be refreshingly novel. She was immediately taken up by the *bon ton*, and on the fringes of the crowded conservatory word was spreading of the discovery of an "Incomparable."

The duchess was delighted. "My dear," she said at one point, "what a treasure you are. You've surpassed all my expectations." Trevenaugh made no comment to Louise, but she was frequently aware of his eyes on her. She carefully avoided meeting his gaze.

She had been talking to a foppish little man about the charms of country living, when she noticed an uncomfortable presence and a demanding stare directed at her. She lifted her head to meet the regard of a tall gentleman who was looking at her with very black, expressionless, and slightly hooded eyes. His face was thin, as were his lips. His cheeks were unnaturally rosy and his hair unnaturally black against his sallow complexion. He bore himself erect, however, and was noteworthy for his elegance in even so splendid a gathering. Louise's interlocutor, noticing that her attention had wandered, turned, and when he saw who she was looking at, he became flustered.

"Good evening, my lord," he said with a nervous and ingratiating laugh. "How agreeable to see you about. How well you are looking, and how—"

"Thank you," the man said with barely moving lips and a noticeable lack of warmth. He did not bother looking at the little fop, but continued staring at Louise as he said, "Perhaps you will be so kind as to introduce us." It was a command rather than a request, and the little man hurried to accommodate.

"Indeed. Indeed. Miss Engleston, may I present Lord Castleton. Lord Castleton is—"

"Thank you," Castleton interrupted, and the little fop ceased to exist.

"I am honored to make your acquaintance, sir," said Louise with a curtsy.

"The honor is entirely mine, ma'am," said Castleton with a bow. Louise regarded him with curious apprehension. He had been so rude to her previous admirer and had dismissed him so brutally, yet having done so he made no further move to ingratiate himself. He seemed to be putting the burden of any exchange they might make on her. She could think of no remark, and was becoming uncomfortable under his stare. She was about to turn away with a smile when he said:

"So you are Louise Engleston, of Twelve Elms."

"Indeed, sir. Do you know Twelve Elms? Have you been there?"

"Never," he said. "But I know the vicinity well. The coast is quite beautiful in those parts."

"Oh, yes, we often consider it superior to Dover as far as view is concerned. . . ." And she prattled on about the scenic delights of the coast until she could think of nothing more to say. Castleton was offering no encouragement, but had lapsed into a wary and watchful silence which made her uneasy. It was as though he were assessing her or taking her measure. When he failed to respond to her last glowing endorsement of the scenic coastline there was a silence which, for Louise, was strained. She smiled, then, and once more was about to turn away when Castleton said:

"I shall have the honor of dancing with you at the ball."

"Thank you, sir. I fear, though, that I do not dance—have not learned any of the dances that I hear are done here, so I would disgrace you in the ballroom." She smiled again, and would have gone to the duchess. She was relieved to see that the diners were being led to the table and that her constrained interview would be finished.

"I shall teach you the dances. They are simple. You will learn quickly." He bowed, turned, and departed for a place near the Prince's chair, leaving Louise surprised and uneasy.

"You seem to have ensnared Lord Castleton," said the duchess, with raised eyebrows, as Louise joined her. "He is very wealthy. You could do much worse."

The remark, which would have reduced Louise to a stammering and blushing girl a few hours earlier, now merely made her laugh—though somewhat embarrassedly—and reply, "I fear he wished to dance with me at the ball, but I had to excuse myself, for I do not know the London dances."

"One need not dance a step to be the belle of the ball, my dear. Do not be discouraged." And she led Louise to the table before she could answer. Seated across from them, but further toward the head of the table, was Trevenaugh. Louise met his regard and smiled. He seemed surprised, then smiled back at her with a little incline of his head.

It was, she thought, the most warmth she had received from him since their meeting.

For the next two hours they were regaled with a succession of delicacies and savories. There were soups and roasts and aspics and salads and sherbets and fruits and cheeses and nuts. It was an assault on Louise's taste buds similar to the one on her sight earlier that day. Finally she was reduced to simply taking a taste of a dish that had been placed before her, and having the rest borne away. It was very wasteful, she reflected—but she noticed that most of the ladies and many of the gentlemen followed the same course. The Prince Regent, however, seemed to finish every plate put before him.

Finally he rose, signaling the end of the dinner, and the ladies retired to freshen themselves for the ball. Louise and the duchess assured each other that they were looking very well, and not a bit fatigued by the dinner. Then they ascended to the ballroom.

The crush was already great when they arrived, but not so great as to obscure the fact that the same care had been lavished on decorations here as in the garden and conservatory. There were flowers and candelabra everywhere, uniting to give a scented glow to the atmosphere. The assemblage seemed even more gracious and splendid than it had below. There was an orchestra at the center

of the long interior wall playing gavottes, but
no one was dancing. Rather there was a great
milling around and a steady hum of chattering voices as friends sought out friends and
the young beaux passed comment on the at-
tributes of the women. The confidence that
Louise had felt earlier waned somewhat under the open scrutiny to which she was subjected, but she was rapidly adapting to the
ways of society, and was able to discern approval in most of the faces turned toward her,
and to ignore any other expressions that
might surface. It was not long before she felt
the same buoyancy and certainty that she had
felt below.

Trevenaugh came to them.

"Henry!" said the duchess. "Are you dancing this evening?"

"It would seem, ma'am, that no one is
dancing this evening," he answered with a
smile, indicating the packed dancing area.

"They will be. It's always this way at the
beginning. His Highness will have the floor
cleared and dancing will begin in no time.
His *fêtes* are always well regulated."

Trevenaugh turned to Louise.

"I hope, ma'am, that you will do me the
honor of being my partner in a set."

"Indeed, sir, the honor would be mine.
But I fear I do not dance, and would make a
sorry and laughable spectacle of myself if I
were to accompany you." Louise truly re-

gretted having to refuse Trevenaugh, for she found his presence increasingly stimulating. He took the refusal with good grace.

"If you stay longer in London than you projected, that is an omission we shall have to correct," he said. He looked as though he would continue the conversation, when there was a hubbub and great press from the center of the room. The floor was being cleared for dancing, and in the confusion Louise was separated from the duchess and Trevenaugh. The first set was announced, and the orchestra began to play.

Louise felt a pressure on her arm, and, thinking to find Trevenaugh or the duchess, she turned with an expectant smile on her lips. She stared into the hooded black eyes of Lord Castleton.

"I have come to claim our dance, ma'am," he said in a low voice, and he gently but very firmly began propelling her toward the dancing area.

Louise tried to resist without making a scene.

"I cannot dance, sir," she said, trying to halt their progress without actually breaking from his grasp. "I fear I would embarrass you if I tried."

"That is my concern, ma'am," he said imperturbably. "I do not embarrass easily."

"Then *I* shall be embarrassed, sir. Please be so kind as to take your hand away," she said with a low voice, and there was a tremor in it. For even though she was surrounded by the most honorable subjects of the realm, she felt terribly helpless. She searched for the duchess or Trevenaugh, but could not find them. Then, suddenly, she found herself part of a set of dancers, with Castleton facing her. She was very angry, and debated whether she should simply walk away. She feared that Castleton would not permit this, and would keep her where he wanted her. All the evening's triumphs fell from her, and once more she felt as helpless as when she had stepped from the coach the day before.

"It is very simple, ma'am. All you need do is follow my movements." He had a firm clasp on her hand as the music began and the couples moved to a slow waltz. Louise hesitantly and reluctantly accommodated herself to the rhythm and flow of Castleton who, it seemed to her, was a superb dancer. After a few minutes she thought how pleasant it would have been to be able to dance had she not been coerced. But she was humiliated and angry at the method Castleton had employed to make her his partner, and pleasure was impossible.

"You see, ma'am, you acquit yourself very well. All you needed was someone to take a firm hand with you," said Castleton, in a low and arrogant tone.

"Your compliment is not welcome, sir. Please return me to my friends."

His response was to increase the pressure on her hand, as he laughed tonelessly.

"But you are just beginning to learn. I have many more steps to teach you."

"Sir, if you do not immediately return me to my friends I shall be forced to ask for help. This is intolerable—you have taken advantage of me and against my will have made me take part in an activity for which I have no appetite."

"On the contrary, your appetite is stronger than one might have thought. See how easily you flow around the floor—so long as you are kept firmly in hand."

The insinuation was palpable, but nonetheless not completely understood by Louise. She was, however, repulsed by the man, who was now holding her more tightly than ever before. It was unthinkable that she should struggle or cry out in this elegant setting—yet she was frightened enough to do so. Castleton's grasp, his gleaming, calculating eyes boring into hers, and the hated, oppressive, heavily scented air surrounding them as they turned and flowed with the rhythms of the waltz—all conspired to heighten Louise's fear and make her feel that she was completely in the power of the man who was so gracefully twirling her around the room.

"This is enough, sir," said Louise. "Return

me to my friends at once." She tried to stop
dancing, but he was too strong, and they continued relentlessly gliding to the music.

"Your father would be very disappointed
in you if he knew you were treating his old
. . . friend . . . so rudely. James Engleston
was ever one for honoring old friendships."

Louise was taken aback. "Why did you
not introduce yourself as a friend of my father, sir? Why did you not make yourself
known to me?"

"Why, because," he said, moving his face
closer to her, so that she could smell the wine
on his breath mingled with the cologne he
was wearing, "because I wanted you to like
me for myself." He smiled, watching her in-
tensely. As with everything else he had done
in her presence, it seemed to Louise that he
meant much more than he was saying.

The music stopped, Castleton released his
grasp, and Louise turned immediately toward
the end of the room. She walked rapidly
without looking back. Just before she reached
the duchess, she felt once more the hateful
pressure on her arm. She turned, frightened
and angry.

Castleton looked unperturbed. "I shall call
on you tomorrow, ma'am," he said.

She opened her mouth to protest, but he
had bowed gracefully and walked away before she could say anything.

She returned to the duchess, who was

watching her curiously. Trevenaugh was at her side, erect, face impassive and colder than she had ever seen it.

"My dear, you accounted for yourself very creditably. I thought you could not dance. But no matter. Now that you find you can, I'm sure you shall not have a spare moment."

"I cannot. Or could not. Lord Castleton . . . led me to the floor under the impression that I was more accomplished than is the fact."

"Ah, yes, Castleton. I hear he can be very persuasive. Among other things. . . . What is it I have heard about Castleton, Henry?" asked the duchess.

Trevenaugh's voice was as unyielding as his demeanor. "I can recall nothing of note ma'am."

"Oh yes, there was something—it will come to me. No matter. He is very rich, and that, of course, is the main thing." She looked at Louise knowingly. "He would be quite a catch, my dear. He is older than I should have liked, but he has kept his figure."

"There is no question of . . . an arrangement being made between us, ma'am. He is simply a friend of my father's. . . ." Louise was appalled at the duchess's misunderstanding. She was made increasingly uncomfortable by the cold presence of Trevenaugh, who would not even look in her direction.

"Well said, my dear. Admit to nothing,"

said the duchess with a chuckle. "How quickly one learns, once she is thrown into society."

Louise decided it was futile to argue. What had begun as a triumphant evening was disintegrating into a series of foolish and embarrassing misconceptions. She wanted nothing so much as to get away.

The music was starting again, and the duchess turned playfully to Trevenaugh. "If you want to dance with this child, Henry, you had better do so now, for she will not be at liberty for long, I fear."

Trevenaugh smiled coldly. "The lady told me she could not dance. I always believe a lady," he said.

The rebuke was so unjust, and so harshly administered that Louise was almost of a mind to answer it. She was, however, unsure of her emotions, and could not trust herself to explain the events of the last few minutes. At that instant she was aware that she wanted Henry Trevenaugh's approbation more than anything, and it seemed impossible to obtain.

She turned to the duchess. "If it would not trouble you too much, ma'am, could I be sent back to your house? I am feeling unwell."

"Of course, child," said the duchess, alarmed, both at her nephew's behavior and the sudden pallor of Louise. "In fact, I am beginning to tire of this *fête* myself, and shall accompany you. Henry, are you staying?"

"For a little while, ma'am, if you will excuse me?"

"Certainly. You will call tomorrow, of course, and we shall begin to seek out young Master Engleston in earnest."

"Of course," he said with a bow to the duchess. He did not look at Louise.

With the duchess leading the way they went to the footman, who summoned their carriage. In a short while they were on their way, and rode mostly in silence.

Louise's only thought was to get away from an atmosphere that, after such a promising start, had suddenly become stifling.

Chapter 6

Josie van Scuyden was giving a reception on the same night the Prince Regent was holding his ball. Several people (though probably not the Prince Regent himself) would have been surprised at how often the two guest lists overlapped. After the more formal festivities at Carlton House, many of the Prince's guests decided to enjoy Josie's less constrained hospitality, and went to her exquisite house at York Place. Though Josie was not as young as some of the other Fashionable Impures, she was still a handsome and vivacious woman. Furthermore, she had enjoyed the protection of the reasonably powerful Lord Fardon for several years—long enough to make the liaison respectable. Her receptions were noteworthy.

It was to Josie's that Castleton went after leaving Carlton House. He arrived late, and there was already the sound of music and laughter floating from the open windows of the grand salon on the second floor. As he was about to ring, a tall, thin, dark figure emerged from the shadows and spoke to him in a low voice.

"If your lordship please."

Castleton turned impatiently and snapped, "What is it, Brombedge?"

"I delivered your message to Mademoiselle de Merivange along with the request for an answer. She kept the message, and told me to tell you she would respond to your note at this reception. I have not been able to find your lordship before now." Brombedge spoke tonelessly, as though he had the information by rote, and was not the least interested in the contents.

Castleton replied in the same fashion. "It was not wise of you, Brombedge, to permit this behavior. I'm surprised, after all these years, you could so lightly disregard my instructions."

"I did everything in my power, sir, to retrieve your note and to persuade her to answer you in writing. She refused. I could not threaten force, for she was entertaining a gentleman who would have bested me in any event."

"No doubt," said Castleton, and smiled at the image of his cadaverous secretary wresting the note from the buxom Cleo de Merivange.

"If you'll permit me, sir, I believe that

Mademoiselle de Merivange aspires to independence. I have seen the signs before."

"You are telling me nothing new, Brombedge. Was there anything else?"

"No, sir, nothing of note."

"Very well, you may go. . . . Oh, Brombedge, have we had word from Engleston at Twelve Elms?"

"No sir, nothing as yet. He is overdue."

"Indeed he is. Remind me to look into that matter tomorrow."

"Yes, sir."

Brombedge watched as Castleton pulled the bell and disappeared into the brightly lighted foyer. Then he turned and started to walk away. Suddenly he bent almost double and, gasping for breath, clutched at the iron railing in front of the house to keep from falling. A spasm passed over his sallow face, and beads of sweat appeared on his forehead and upper lip. He spent a long minute doubled over, his eyes tightly shut, his breath coming in gasps. Little by little the attack seemed to subside, and after a few minutes he straightened and proceeded down the road, though more slowly and hesitantly than before.

Castleton stepped into the brilliant foyer, awash with the sounds of laughter and music, and gave his hat, cane, and gloves to the waiting footman. Then he proceeded up the stairs directly to the grand salon. He walked casually, perfectly at ease. His carriage was erect and the tilt of his head indicated a bored arrogance. His eyes flicked from face to face, and occasionally he would nod very slightly when some acquaintance came into sight.

At the entrance of the salon he was greeted effusively by Josie, who was done up in white satin and diamonds and more ostrich feathers than it seemed possible for one woman to wear.

"Lord Castleton! Now my little gathering is complete. It wanted only you to make it a success."

"You are a flatterer, my dear Madame van Scuyden. And that is not the least reason why I am here." He kissed her hand.

"Impossible to flatter you, my lord. A few honest and deserved compliments might sound like flattery—but that's because you are so modest." She took her hand away from his and indicated the filled salon with a grand sweep of her arm.

"Enter! Enter and be entertained, my lord. Surely you will find something to amuse you at my little party."

Castleton bowed and walked into the throng of chattering people. Many of the men had been seen earlier at the Prince's ball. The women, however, were all completely fresh and were, on the whole, younger and more picturesquely garbed. Many of them—a surprising proportion—were exquisite, and all were more animated and seemed more accessible than those seen at Carlton House.

Castleton walked slowly, and apparently without aim, among the guests. Occasionally he would return a greeting, but in such a way as to discourage any further conversation. He strolled the length of the room, and was preparing to return on the other side when he spied a mass of gleaming golden curls through a group of attentive gentlemen. Cleo was regaling them with the latest gossip.

" . . . so the poor duke has had to give up his Mary Ann and retire to the country with his duchess who has, they say, over one hundred pet dogs. Not a one of them a thoroughbred. But then, after Mary Ann, the duke is accustomed to . . . mongrels . . . and should feel at home, wouldn't you say?" There was laughter as Cleo spied Castleton watching her. Her expression changed from malicious gaiety to a watchful and feline smile.

"Why, there is Lord Castleton! What a pleasure to see you, my lord." She advanced and took his arm. "Come, tell me your news—it's been so long since I've had the pleasure of chatting with you."

"A pleasure indeed, my dear Cleo. You are ravishing this evening. It must be that you have a new protector—or perhaps the rumor I heard that it is you who are now doing the protecting is true, and it is some young man who has brought this glow to your cheeks."

Cleo's eyes narrowed, and her smile grew more set.

"Ah, Castleton, you have always been a tease."

"A tease? Possibly. I have never, though, been a fool—I believe?" He asked the question in the same lighthearted tone that Cleo had used, but his eyes showed no mirth.

"Certainly not, my dear Castleton. Why? Has someone accused you of being a fool?" Cleo asked. Her head was held high, and she turned to Castleton with an insolent smile.

"Oh no, no one would dare *accuse* me. There are those, however, who might be misled into *treating* me as such." He laughed and patted her hand on his arm.

"Surely you have nothing to fear from such benighted souls?"

"I am not speaking from fear, my dear, but from concern. I should hate to have to discipline someone whose welfare has been my preoccupation these last few years."

"Come to the point, Castleton." Cleo's smile was unchanged, but her eyes were hard as agates.

"Why did you treat my secretary so lightly, and disregard my instruction?"

"What has Brombedge told you?" Cleo asked, her eyes widened in feigned surprise.

"He must have delivered my message . . . or you wouldn't be here."

"As it happens, I was coming here regardless . . . but that is beside the point. Why did you keep my note, when I asked its return, and why did you not reply as requested? I have reason for these little idiosyncrasies, my dear."

"I know your reasons, Castleton." Cleo's voice was abrupt. "I have no intention of adding my letters to your collection—particularly as regards the . . . matter . . . at hand. As for keeping yours—well, it seems wise to keep some specimen of yours nearby as a precaution.

Castleton looked off into the distance, a smile lingering on his lips.

"To think that you would not trust me after all these years," he said musingly. "Are you forgetting that I know more about you than you know yourself? That it was I who found a filthy little prison urchin named Sadie Mudd, and transformed her into a Cleo de Merivange? That it was I who advised her in all her affairs—from the besotted Duke of Arguise to that fool Trevenaugh—are you forgetting all this, Sadie?"

"Don't call me that," Cleo hissed between her teeth. She composed herself then, and her smile returned to her lips.

"I am forgetting nothing. Nothing. I remember that the man who found the child in debtor's prison was well rewarded for the transformation he effected. He could have saved that child with generosity and created an entirely different woman from the one he selfishly wanted for his own purposes."

"Come, come. Are you telling me that child would rather have been a governess, say, or retired to a convent? Or perhaps would rather have been handed over to some good burgher as his little wife? I do not see you as a tavernkeeper's wife, my dear Cleo."

"I am simply saying that whatever you have given me has been well repaid, Castleton. I am astonished that you should seek perpetual gratitude from me."

"I am seeking only our mutual benefit," said Castleton smoothly. "We can be of enormous aid to each other, provided we act with trust."

Cleo was silent for a few moments, smiling sweetly and thinking furiously.

At last she said, "But what is all this talk of lack of trust? Of course I trust you—how could it be otherwise?"

"How, indeed, my dear?" said Castleton drily.

Cleo continued. "I do think, though, that in our present undertaking we should eschew notes and messages. If there is any intelligence that must be exchanged, let us meet."

"As we are meeting now, my dear."

"Yes. Your note mentioned an important

visitor—but wisely named no names. Is this someone I shall be receiving before long?"

"Possibly. You might hear from him at any moment—that is why I wished to alert you."

"This is a dangerous game, Castleton."

"But the reward is very high, my dear. You are receiving more than triple what you might receive for some of your other services."

There was an undercurrent of scorn in his voice that piqued Cleo. She pursed her lips and narrowed her eyes; then on an impulse she extended her left arm in order to display an emerald and diamond bracelet.

"Tell me, Castleton, do you like this?" she said, looking at him through her long lashes.

"Pretty," he said, annoyed at her changing the subject.

"I could wish you were capable of more enthusiasm," she laughed. "After all, this bracelet is, in a sense, a gift from you."

Castleton looked again and warily said, "I don't follow you."

"Why, I have just learned that this gift was bought with money that was intended for you," Cleo said with a laugh.

"What sort of game are you playing, Cleo? You are trying my patience."

"Oh, then, I shall be more explicit. Do you know a Mr. Engleston from Twelve Elms?" Cleo was gratified to see the start of surprise on Castleton's face. He had cultivated impassiveness with such success that she had abandoned any hope of ever seeing him show any emotion. The slight change of his expression told her that she had hit upon something more valuable than she had surmised.

"The name is familiar," he said, once more controlled and inscrutable.

"I should think it would be very familiar, Castleton. He owes you money, I believe?"

Castleton turned a cool gaze on her, but said nothing.

"Or perhaps I am mistaken. Perhaps it is another Engleston. Let us drop the whole matter. Silly of me to bring it up."

Castleton smiled coldly. "Continue your story, Cleo."

"Oh, I didn't think you were interested. Well, it seems this Engleston of Twelve Elms has been in the habit of bringing money up to London every year to be delivered to a certain *personnage*. This year he was not feeling well, so he sent his young son instead. The boy is very pretty, very untried, unused to the ways of town, and so when he arrived he chanced to fall into the company of a beautiful and kind woman who took him under her wing and initiated him into the ways of the world. In gratitude, this young and very pretty lad decided to make his friend a gift. Only he had no money of his own. All he had was the sum that had been intended for the *personnage*. Being a lad of spirit, love overcame his scruples, and he spent that sum for his beautiful lady friend."

"A very touching story. I take it he bought his friend a bracelet?"

"Perceptive, Castleton."

"And what happened to this pretty lad? Having exhausted his capital, I suppose he was no longer considered quite so attractive, and the beautiful woman sent him back to the country."

"Ah, if you believe that it is because you do not understand that in addition to being beautiful and kind, the lady is very good. She would never toss aside a pretty lad simply for lack of funds."

"Possibly I have not followed this story as closely as I might. The beautiful lady I had in mind would not only toss aside a pretty lad, she would—if necessary—even turn her back on her own father, and let him rot to pieces in debtor's prison without lifting a hand."

Cleo's smile disappeared and her eyes narrowed. "That was on your advice, Castleton."

"I *advised*, yes. After all, he was not *my* father. I did not coerce you, however. But we digress. Continue your story, my dear."

"The story is finished."

"Not quite. What happened to the pretty lad?"

"I weary of this game."

"I begin to savor it. Where is the pretty lad? Let me guess. . . . Why, I wager he is among us at this very moment. Am I correct?"

Cleo said nothing. She had grown sullen; her mouth was set and she stared at the floor.

"Come, Cleo, it is rather late to express filial regret. Your father was a brute, and deserved more than he got. He should have been hanged."

"Then why do you throw him in my face?"

"I merely mentioned it in passing, my dear. I mentioned it in the spirit of our little game. I had no intention of throwing it in your face."

"You have no feelings, Castleton, and you treat others as though they were as bloodless as you."

"My dear, let us not enter a discussion of this sort. It could prove tedious. Let us return to your story. It interests me, I confess. I should like to know if young Engleston is here now?"

"Yes."

"Ah. I do not wish to meet him at the moment. But I find his presence very interesting. Your charming story, charmingly told, has pleasantly diverted me. But now we must put aside our games and proceed to other considerations. I mentioned a visitor. . . ." His voice lowered and Cleo's sullenness gradually gave way to attention. Together they strolled slowly out onto the terrace.

Charles had watched Cleo all evening. Though he was too far away to hear what was being said, he knew that the tall, slender man with the unnaturally black hair and rosy cheeks must be Lord Castleton, and he felt a clutch of anguish in the pit of his stomach. He was repelled both by the man and by himself, for having got in this man's power. He was overwhelmed with guilt and with flashes of hatred for Cleo. Yet when he saw, at one point, that she seemed distressed, he had to suppress an urge to rush to her and assure her that he would protect her. And when he saw her stroll slowly to the terrace on Castleton's arm, he was struck with suspicion and jealousy so intense that he thought he must follow them. Possibly he would have done so had he not been interrupted by a low musical voice.

– "I beg your pardon, sir, but I am having difficulty with my fan. Could you hold my champagne a moment . . . ?" The speaker was a small auburn-haired woman—probably no more than nineteen or twenty—who, without being beautiful, was nonetheless alluring. Her shoulders were bare, and her dress was very décolleté. She smiled at Charles, simulating shyness, and held her glass of champagne to him.

"With pleasure, ma'am," said Charles stiffly. Though he had been to several gatherings similar to this one in the past three months, he had not learned how to flirt and had the disarming trait of taking everything anybody said at face value. He dutifully held the champagne while the young woman fussed with her fan, opening and closing it, with many upward glances at Charles, who stood disinterestedly by.

Finally she seemed satisfied that the fan worked and, smiling, she said, "Thank you *so* much. It is such a warm evening, and with a broken fan a girl could possibly swoon from the heat."

Charles handed her the champagne. "Yes, ma'am, I suppose that is possible," he said. The young girl hesitated, then shrugged her shoulders and moved away. Charles renewed his watch on the terrace door.

He did not notice the haughty, dark man who had been watching him from a short distance, and who had, with some amusement, witnessed the scene that had just been played. The man now came to him and said:

"Sir. You are Charles Engleston, I believe." His tone and manner immediately put Charles on the defensive.

"That is correct. And whom have I the

pleasure of addressing?" he asked, trying for, but not achieving, an arrogance that would be commensurate with that of the stranger.

"I am Henry Trevenaugh. I have come to you with a message from your sister."

Chapter 7

After a fretful night, Louise awoke still feeling depressed and apprehensive. She had run such a gamut of emotions the evening before—from budding confidence to triumph to fear to humiliation—that it seemed she had compressed a lifetime into a few hours. She had returned with the duchess, who had been sympathetic but had found nothing consoling to say—had seemed, in fact, at a loss for words about Trevenaugh's behavior. They had parted at the staircase, and Louise had retired immediately.

Now it was morning. She could tell because of the racket being made by the servants and on the street. Louise reflected that silence seemed to be the one luxury that could not be obtained in London. She wanted to leave the city and return to Twelve Elms, where the life might be dull (she had not realized just how dull until the last two days), but it was also safe and reassuring. She longed for the certitude that familiar surroundings could give her and the comfort that being with her father and Charles and Agatha could bring. At the thought of Charles she sighed. She had been in London now for two full days (only two days!) but had come no closer to finding his whereabouts than when she was at Twelve Elms. She was living in ducal splendor. Somewhere, possibly not far, Charles was living—how? She refused to follow the thought through. She determined to take steps to find him and to return to Twelve Elms with him today. She decided that she could no longer indulge herself by living out the duchess's fantasies—for that was what seemed to be happening—and must firmly return to reality. Reality was, very simply, that she was a young country girl, of decent family, who had come to London seeking her brother. She had no business lying in this splendid bed, nor attending balls at Carlton House and hobnobbing with dukes—particularly such arrogant and superior dukes as Trevenaugh. She had a duty to her father to find Charles and return to Twelve Elms straightaway.

Upon that firm resolution she rose and went about her toilet. When it came time to dress, she was going to put on her own cotton frock that she had traveled in. But the sight of the rose silk morning dress proved too much for her resolve, and she slipped into it as naturally as a fish into water. It was like wearing scented air, and she thought, ruefully, that she would miss it when she left the duchess's house. She carefully applied a little of the salves and lotions to her face, as well as just the smallest suspicion of tint to her lips. She studied the effect, and once more decided that she was indeed a different person here than at Twelve Elms.

She descended to the breakfast room, where the same lavish array of food awaited her as on the preceding morning. Once again it seemed almost wicked to Louise that so much should be prepared for just two women—the eggs and the meats and porridges and breads and rolls were all displayed in different quantity to feed the whole establishment at Twelve Elms, including the seasonal hands. The sideboard was gleaming with silver dishes and trays and crystal bowls and goblets, all filled with mounds of food and sparkling liquids. She helped herself to a few spoonfuls of eggs and a small roll.

As the footman was bringing her tea, the duchess entered. She seemed to have regained all her aplomb during the night, and was in excellent spirits.

"My dear! Up and about! How fortunate. I thought I should have to await all the morning until you should be coaxed from your bed, after your triumph of last evening. We have a world of things to accomplish to-

day, and the sooner we get started the better."
The duchess was moving down the sideboard
like a fastidious bird, scooping up spoonfuls
of delicacies with quick, sure gestures. She
handed her filled plate to the footman, who
carried it to the table. "First we must make
some calls and consolidate your victory.
Many women are most anxious to meet this
season's Incomparable, and if you are
gracious—as I'm sure you will be—you can
make some very useful friends . . . for the
season, at least. A girl can't have too many
useful friends when she's after a husband."

As the duchess talked on, Louise became
more distressed. She stiffened her spine and set
her jaw, however, and spoke quietly:

"Ma'am, I fear I cannot join you in making calls today. I must find my brother and
return to Twelve Elms as soon as it is feasi-
ble. I hope I can find him today, in fact. I
appreciate your kindness—it is more than I
deserve. But I really cannot take advantage
of it any longer. I should appreciate your
advising me as to how best I might find
Charles. . . . Perhaps I should, after all, call
upon this . . . lady . . . who has ensnared
him." She was blushing, but her purpose remained unshaken.

The duchess was amused. "But my dear, of
course we shall find your brother. Henry is
occupying himself with that quest. As for
calling on Cleo de Merivange, the idea is ab-

surd, my child—unthinkable. You were seen
last night chatting with His Highness, the
Prince Regent, by all of London. Do you
want it bruited about that you were seen today in the company of one of His Majesty's
less savory subjects? Your brother Charles can
cavort with her as he likes, and his reputation will be enhanced. But *you*, my dear,
would be ruined if you were so much as to
exchange comments about the weather with
her. Now, enough of this nonsense about calling on Cleo de Merivange. We shall simply
have to let circumstances take their course.
It might be that Henry can contact your
brother today. Well and good. It might even
be that you can return to your home today.
But wouldn't it be even more satisfying to
return home not only with a lost brother, but
also with a newfound and rich husband?
While you are here, my dear, take advantage
of what Providence has sent your way. You
have been well launched in the season. You
will have offers. I shall see to it."

"But ma'am, I don't want a husband . . .
or at least that is not what I came to London
for. I have no plans whatsoever concerning
matrimony—"

"Child, child. What else is there for you?
Of course you want a husband—you have just
not yet been made aware of the desire for
one. I have been sent by a kindly fate to
remedy that lack. As for this missing brother,

he is in the process of being found. There is nothing more you can do in that area. Why not employ your time to advantage, and let us set about getting you married and married well."

The duchess spoke with such conviction that Louise saw it would be useless to argue. Since she had been assured that Tevenaugh was looking for Charles, there was nothing more she could do. She had no place to go. She had no choice but to cooperate with the duchess.

"Indeed, ma'am, I don't know how to respond to your concern. . . . You must forgive me if I seem ungrateful. I am—"

A footman entered and said to the duchess:

"Lord Castleton is here to see Miss Engleston, Your Grace."

"So early!" said the duchess. "What did I tell you, my dear? And I am sure he will be only the first of many. I wish he could be a little younger . . . but it would be sinfully greedy of me to wish he could be richer—for he is very rich indeed. Now, how do you look? . . . Well, of course, lovely . . . have you finished your breakfast? Yes. Ordinarily I should accompany you for the meeting, but I think I will be daring and let you pass a little time alone with Castleton. Then I shall come in later and be surprised to find him there. We musn't let on we expected him."

There was no question of Louise's having to feign surprise. She was not only surprised, she was also chilled at the announcement that Castleton had, as he had said he would, called on her.

"If you please, ma'am, I do not wish to be alone with Lord Castleton. He frightens me, and I do not trust him."

"Frightens you? Of course he does. You must learn to overcome that fear. After all, my dear, you are playing a new game—and the stakes are very high. I don't doubt that you are frightened. But the fear will pass once the game has been played a few times. Castleton will be, if nothing else, practice for you."

"I fear you misunderstand me, ma'am. I find Lord Castleton objectionable. He said things last night that should not have been said."

The duchess was very interested. "Did he make improper suggestions, my dear?"

"No, ma'am. Not really improper . . . but he . . . seemed to be implying things—"

The duchess trilled into laughter. "Oh, my dear. He was *flirting*. You are unaccustomed to ways among the *ton*. He would have been rude not to flirt. You must put aside your country prejudices and indulge our city gentlemen. Of course he was implying things. *You* must imply things also—but state no facts. That is the art to be developed."

With a sinking heart Louise saw that she would not be able to convince the duchess that Castleton was sinister, and that the fear she felt was not simply that of a young girl making her social debut. It was fear that stemmed from the presence of a tangible threat. To have stated such a fear in the duchess's well-appointed dining room, surrounded with servants and under the lively eye of the duchess herself, would have been an absurdity. There was no possibility of explaining herself. With a bow and a murmured agreement, Louise went into the drawing room alone.

Castleton was standing in front of the fireplace, facing the door. When she entered he smiled and advanced to greet her.

"Good morning, ma'am. It is an even greater pleasure to see you again than I had anticipated." He reached for her hand, but she withdrew it. After a moment's hesitation he shrugged and regarded her ironically. "I took the liberty of calling so early because I knew that, being from the country, you would doubtless be an early riser—as am I."

"Good morning, sir. It . . . is kind of you to call," said Louise. She walked to an isolated chair and sat in it. Castleton pulled one of the small gilt chairs near and sat facing her, his knees almost touching hers.

He leaned forward, bringing his face near

hers, and asked, "What do you know of me, ma'am?"

Louise recoiled from his thrusting face. "Indeed, sir, nothing at all, except that you profess to a friendship with my father."

"Come now, you are not so innocent as all that. You have surely learned something about me?"

"No, sir, I have not." Louise found his questions, and the manner of putting them, preposterous.

"The Duchess of Bledrough is very canny. She must have told you something about me?"

Louise remembered that the duchess had stated that he was wealthy, but she thought it would be improper to mention that. "Sir, I do not know what you are talking about, and I find this conversation distasteful." She started to rise, but he reached out for her arm and forced her back into the seat.

"Be patient, ma'am. You will soon find the conversation very much to your taste."

Louise experienced again the fear she had felt with him the night before at the ball, when he had used force to make her continue waltzing against her will. She shrank from his touch and tried to struggle free.

"Sir, this is obnoxious behavior. Take your hands off me."

"Not until we have had our chat. I have important things to say to you, and you will have important issues to ponder before we are finished. Now then, you are quite sure that the Duchess of Bledrough has told you nothing about me?"

Louise briefly thought of not replying at all, in the hopes of discouraging his inquisition. But his manner was so intense and persistent that she decided such a course would be futile.

"As I told you, sir, I know nothing about you except that you profess a friendship with my father, a profession I am more and more disinclined to believe in view of your treatment of me. Please remove your hands at once or I shall call for a servant."

"Call for a servant, by all means," he chuckled. "But your best interest is to hear me out." He did take his hands from her arms, however, and sat back in his chair. "Now then, perhaps I had better tell you what I was sure by now you knew. I am a very wealthy man."

He looked at Louise's perplexed expression expectantly. When he saw that she was not going to speak, he continued.

"I am a very good match for some lucky girl." Louise regarded him with growing astonishment.

"I have decided that it is time for me to take a wife—my station in life demands it." Louise continued to regard him, silently.

"With my resources I have an extraordinary choice of prospects, of course. However, my standards are high—though not in the sense that society might understand." He paused significantly. "What I demand from a spouse is very much out of fashion nowadays, I believe."

Louise continued listening with growing dread. She felt that she should stop the conversation, but did not know how. She could think of no way to stem the flood of Castleton's confidences.

"I have never been daunted by any lack," he continued. "When I have needed something, and it has not been readily available to me, I have created it. Always with remarkable success. Now I need a wife of a sort that is in very short supply, if she exists at all. So I shall have to create one that is suitable to my needs." He paused and looked at Louise appraisingly.

"The women who move in my circle have become too independent and opinionated. They are about in public places too much unaccompanied. It is not unusual for a woman of *ton* to be seen with a man other than her husband. These women have come to accept such behavior as their right. I do not approve. My wife—like Caesar's—shall be above reproach, not because I shall continue to insist upon it, but because she will be taught to be so inclined. Do you follow me?"

Louise was very still for a few seconds,

trying to think of some way to extricate herself from this situation. She obliquely regarded the intense man facing her, his sallow complexion highlighting his glistening piercing eyes, the unnaturally black hair, and (she could see now) the rouged cheeks. She was repelled by him physically and, at the same time, she was as frightened as if he were some poisonous serpent that was preparing to coil around her helpless body. When she spoke it was with a very small voice.

"This is not a conversation that is suitable for us, sir. I beg you to excuse me now."

He smiled and looked at her appreciatively. "And of course," he said, "this wife of mine must have spirit, a mind and character. In order for me to create something worthwhile I must have suitable raw material. After all, nothing comes from nothing, as Lear said to Cordelia."

He leaned toward her. "You have been raised in the country, ma'am. You have seen wild horses broken. The more spirited, the more difficult the training, the more splendid the result. A fine, mettlesome unfettered beast makes—with proper training—a gentle, sturdy domesticated friend to man. The training is all."

Louise realized the absurdity of the comparison. Far from feeling like a spirited horse, she felt like a threatened rabbit longing for its warren. She prayed that someone would interrupt them.

"I need a wife, ma'am. She must be beautiful, of good—though not necessarily aristocratic—breeding, and she must be intelligent and possess character. I am capable of making a quick judgment, both of men and matters. Though I have known you a scant few hours, I am certain that you fill all my requirements. In short, Miss Engleston, I am offering you marriage."

He sat back with a smile, and watched her. Louise waited, hoping for something to happen that would eliminate the need for a response. The silence became more tense and Castleton's smile more fixed.

"Perhaps, sir, there was something in my manner that led you to believe I should welcome such a proposal. If that is the case, I am sorry—"

"No, ma'am, there was nothing of the sort in your manner. Had there been, I should have considered you too forward and bold, and the proposal would not have been made."

"Sir, I cannot accept."

"You are simply overcome, and need time to think."

"I need no time, sir. I can tell you now that I reject your offer."

"Nonsense. You would be a fool to follow such a course. You are not a fool, or I never would have chosen you to be my wife. You are doubtless overwhelmed by your good fortune."

Castleton's arrogance and absolute certainty that she would be grateful for his offer fanned her smoldering resentment into full flame. She rose violently from her chair and stood facing him.

"Nothing, sir, could induce me to be your wife. I need no time, no further consideration. You have not honored but insulted me by your offer. Last night you forced me to dance against my will. Today, not more than a quarter of an hour ago, you restrained me violently from leaving you. Now you seem intent upon using the same force to make me your wife. It will not come to pass, sir. I am not a horse to be trained according to your dictates. I repeat, for you seem uncommonly impervious to my words, that I will not be your wife under any circumstances. Now, sir, please leave me."

Castleton listened to her speech with growing annoyance. He did not move from his chair, but sat looking at her until she was finished.

"Be careful, ma'am. Spirit is one thing. Insolence is another. Your conduct is bordering on the latter."

"Can you not understand, sir, that I have no interest in your judgment of my conduct? Can you not understand that I abhor the sight of you? Leave me, sir, this instant."

"You are becoming hysterical, ma'am, and are saying things you will later regret. I urge you to calm yourself before you commit some foolishness that will make our union unnecessarily difficult."

"Sir, there is to be no union!" Louise was, indeed, beginning to feel hysterical in the face of Castleton's total disregard of her wishes and statements.

"You are mistaken, ma'am. There *will* be a union, and soon." Castleton was no longer smiling, but he continued to sit seemingly at ease and regard Louise through half-closed eyes.

Exasperated, she turned wordlessly to leave the room. She had taken only a few steps when Castleton stopped her by saying:

"If you value your father it would be very unwise for you to leave."

Louise turned to him. "How dare you flaunt your friendship for my father in such circumstances?"

Castleton smiled. "I am not speaking of friendship. I am speaking of more practical matters. Such as life and death."

Louise was stunned by the deadly fixed stare from the unsmiling eyes. Though her impulse was to run as far away from Castleton as she could, she was restrained by a mixture of curiosity and fear. She tried to put a brave front on the matter by asking as sharply as possible, "What do you mean? Explain yourself."

Castleton seemed in no hurry to comply. He looked at his hands carefully, as though engrossed in their inspection. When he finally spoke it was in a musing, abstracted manner. "Your father is considered an honorable man in your parts, I believe."

"My father *is* an honorable man. His reputation is stainless."

Castleton raised his eyes to her and smiled ironically. "Does he prattle on about honor—that of his good name and his children's good name, et cetera?"

"He does not prattle about that or anything else. You are being insulting."

"Not insulting. Merely descriptive."

"You profess to friendship with my father, yet you malign him to his daughter. You are not acting in good faith."

"I have never, I believe, mentioned 'friendship.' That was your contribution. I do not claim your father's friendship—although I might have cultivated it had I known I would one day be marrying his daughter."

Louise nearly gasped at the insolent disregard for facts. "I am not going to marry you," she said through clenched teeth.

"Yes, my dear, you are. If you don't, you will be seeing your father swing from a gibbet."

His manner lost the arrogant, deadly playfulness. He was unsmiling and his eyes glimmered with triumph. The words and the tone—which bore an all-too-real conviction—struck Louise like a blow. She was still for a minute, trying to regain her balance, then found she had to sit down. She stared at Castleton all the while, and he at her.

"I do not understand," she said.

"That's because I choose that you not understand. Yet. When the time comes for more facts, rest assured that I shall produce them. Until such a time I advise you to listen rather more sympathetically to my courtship." He spoke the last word ironically.

Louise had grown white and still. It was evident that this was no ruse, but a real threat. All her instincts, from her first meeting with Castleton, had warned her to avoid him. She had sensed danger and threat in his presence. Now she knew that her instincts had been correct. There was a great power for evil in Castleton. In some way he was able to manipulate her father and herself like puppets. It was just this lack of precise knowledge about how he was able to do so that gave her fear such a sharp edge.

The door to the drawing room opened, and Trevenaugh entered. He paused at the threshold, and immediately sensed the tension. He looked quickly from Louise to Castleton, and then back to Louise with a trace of concern in his regard.

"Good morning, Trevenaugh," said Castleton, thoroughly at his ease.

Trevenaugh nodded coldly. Then he turned back to Louise's frightened white face and said,

"Are you troubled, ma'am?"

"I..."

"Not a bit of it," said Castleton insolently. "We were just having a little chat about a mutual acquaintance. I have been fortunate enough to glean some moments alone with Miss Engleston—the first precious harbinger of many more to come, I trust." He smiled at both Louise and Trevenaugh, who greeted his speech with, respectively, looks of dread and dislike.

Trevenaugh repeated to Louise, "Are you troubled, ma'am? Can I help you?"

"Miss Engleston is somewhat overwrought by a very intense discussion we have had— one that affects both her and my future in a most personal manner." Castleton was almost coy.

Trevenaugh looked from one to the other, his expression changing from concern to contempt. "Then I beg your pardon for interrupting," he said coldly and started to withdraw.

"Not at all," said Castleton. "In fact, I must be leaving, myself." He turned to Louise. "I must go now, but with your permission, I shall return tomorrow and we can continue our discussion." His voice was full of innuendo.

Louise realized what it must sound like to Trevenaugh, who was watching the performance disdainfully, standing to one side. Yet she could not forbid Castleton to come again. She was still so frightened about his power over her father that she was trembling. She dared not inflame him to exercise it by going against his wishes. She regarded him mutely. Both he and Trevenaugh intepreted the silence as acquiesence.

"Delightful," said Castleton. He stood up and advanced toward her. He took her lifeless hand, raised it to his lips, "Until tomorrow, then," he said. He nodded to Trevenaugh and left.

The silence he left behind him was oppressive. Louise wanted to unburden herself, but one look at Trevenaugh's cold, withdrawn face told her that it was useless to expect a receptive hearing from him. He had seen her last night dancing with Castleton, after she had refused his invitation. Now he found her, the next morning, alone with Castleton, and in a most agitated state. What else could he think but that they had reached an understanding?

If Trevenaugh had shown even a suspicion of warmth, something akin to his earlier concern when he had entered the room, Louise would have rushed to gain his protection. She was so terribly alone that she would have crossed the barriers of decorum and openly begged for his sympathy. But just because he was the one person whose esteem meant the most to her, he was precisely the person to whom she could not risk showing weakness.

Since Trevenaugh did not seem inclined to break the silence, Louise was going to leave the drawing room, when the duchess entered.

"Well. Here we all are. But where's Lord Castleton, my dear? Has he gone so soon? Henry, how long have you been here? I hope you did not interrupt an important discussion between Castleton and our visitor?" Louise blushed at this allusion to what must have sounded like a matchmaking conspiracy to Trevenaugh. The situation was more and more painful.

"I have just arrived, ma'am," said Trevenaugh coldly.

"What a morning this has been," said the duchess gaily, eyes sparkling. She turned to Louise. "My dear, we already have invitations for tonight. We must choose carefully. What was the result of your little meeting with Castleton?"

"There was no result, ma'am. As for tonight, if you remember, you promised me that you would help me to find Charles—"

"Ah yes," said the duchess, "we must dispose of that tiresome brother of yours. Henry, have you found him?"

"I have found him," Trevenaugh said to Louise. "I talked to him last night. He is unable to call upon you today because of some previous commitment. He shall see you tomorrow at the earliest." He spoke with detachment, hardly bothering to look at her.

"There. You see, my child, nothing simpler. What did I tell you? And while we are waiting for the young man to come around, we shall amuse ourselves this evening."

All Louise wanted was to be away from London. She was grateful to hear of Charles's discovery, and turned to Trevenaugh to acknowledge his role in it. But he refused to look at her, and seemed engrossed in the details of an urn that he must have seen a thousand times. She could not understand, however, why Charles would not come to her immediately. His lack of response was so disquieting that it canceled out her relief at hearing of him.

"Was he . . . in good health?" asked Louise timidly.

"Splendid, I should say. He appeared quite robust," said Trevenaugh without turning from the urn.

"Then . . . I do not understand the delay," said Louise.

"Nor do I," said Trevenaugh curtly. "I

am merely relaying a message. I have no interpretations to offer."

The duchess looked momentarily distressed, then thoughtful, and paused a moment before she said, "But no matter. He has been found. Now we must all be about our business. My dear, let us go to some shops to round out whatever little furbelows you still require."

Louise left the drawing room to fetch her shawl and bonnet. As she was entering her room she met what looked like a parade of servants bearing boxes and packages. These were, she was told, some more of her gowns and accessories from Madame Lucille. The rest would be delivered in two days. It seemed to Louise that she was being inextricably attached to a way of life for which she had an ever-diminishing allegiance.

Chapter 8

Charles awoke the morning after Josie van Scuyden's reception feeling tired and knowing that something was wrong. It was only a few seconds before the cause of his uneasiness appeared before him like an evil spirit, as he remembered having met the handsome and arrogant man who told him that his sister was in London looking for him. Their exchange had been abrupt and strained, rather like a fencing match, with Charles on the defensive.

"I am Henry Trevenaugh," the stranger had said. "I have come to you with a message from your sister."

The news made Charles's heart lurch, and all the guilt about having betrayed the trust of his father had become unmasked and stared nakedly at him. The stranger's manner had been so aloof and so lacking in warmth that Charles had responded with a newly acquired but still unconvincing arrogance.

"From my sister, sir? You come recently from Twelve Elms, then?"

"I come recently from no further than Carlton House, which is where I left your sister no more than an hour ago."

"Louise at Carlton House!" Charles exclaimed, unable to maintain the veneer he had been at such pains to establish. "How did she come to be there?"

"She is there under the protection of my aunt. She has come to London in search of you, sent by your father."

Blood suffused Charles's face, and he was unable for several moments to meet the stranger's eye. When he did gain control of himself he resumed the conversation with an even greater degree of insolence than before.

"And may I ask what circumstance has involved you in our family's affairs?"

"Accident, sir, I assure you."

"I don't follow you."

"No reason why you should. Suffice it to say that your sister is staying with my aunt, the Duchess of Bledrough, and will welcome a visit from you at your earliest convenience."

Charles could not face a meeting with Louise in which he would have to admit that he had betrayed their father. He thought that if only he could have time, there might be a way to erase the past three months and set his life to rights again. Yet he wanted to see her.

A wave of homesickness swept over him, and so intense was his longing that he thought he might cry. He covered these conflicting feelings with a canopy of bluster.

"I am not free tomorrow, unfortunately. You may tell my sister, however, that I shall be happy to wait upon her the following day."

Trevenaugh nodded almost imperceptibly and smiled very slightly.

"Very well," was all he said. He started to leave, but was stopped by a musical greeting and touch on his arm.

"Why it's Henry Trevenaugh, back from the wilderness," said Cleo. She had returned from the terrace unaccompanied, and stood before Trevenaugh smiling coquettishly and knowingly. "Back from the wilderness," she repeated, "but having acquired some rather rough manners, apparently. I cannot explain otherwise why you have not been to see me."

Trevenaugh's back had become ramrod stiff, and his expression more closed. "Good evening, ma'am," he said.

"Ma'am? Now I know you have been consorting with savages. Ma'am, indeed. Since when do you talk to old friends with such formality?" Cleo was enjoying herself. Her eyes were narrowed with the same sort of pleasure to be seen in the expression of a cat with a mouse. Charles sensed the undercurrent between them, and this added to his general misery.

Trevenaugh smiled coldly and left without another word.

"Who is that fellow?" Charles asked Cleo, trying to appear indifferent.

"That, my pet, is now the Duke of Wickenshire. The title is recent. He is very handsome, don't you think?"

Instantly the jealousy that was never very far from the surface of Charles's being flamed up.

"He is not a very agreeable person, I thought. As for his looks, he is rather too stiff and cold."

Cleo smiled and took his chin in her hand. "Don't worry, Charlie, he's not nearly as handsome as you," she said, as though soothing an infant. He recognized the condescension in her voice, but was so grateful for the attention that he bore it without complaint.

They had left the reception together shortly after that, and had returned to Cleo's house. It was a rare privilege, of late, for Charles to be allowed to be so long with Cleo, and he had been transported by her affection and tenderness toward him. For all that, he had not been allowed to spend the whole night in Cleo's silver barque-shaped bed, but had to retire to another chamber because she said she was capable of sleeping well only when she was alone. So Charles had slept by himself, fitfully, with apprehension constantly nipping at the edges of his consciousness. Now he awoke, feeling uneasy.

He stretched and rose, and dressed. He wandered out of his chamber in the direction of Cleo's boudoir. None of the servants were about. After tapping gently at the door, he entered, even though there had been no reply. The drapes were drawn and he could see that Cleo was still sleeping. He longed to awaken her, but was restrained by the fear of displeasing her. He quietly withdrew and descended the stairs.

He had not discussed Lord Castleton with Cleo last night, for he had not wanted any disagreeableness to mar their hours together. He thought that he would see later today whether Cleo and Castleton had discussed the money he owed the latter. He hoped that some solution to his disgrace would be found. As soon as it was taken care of he would go to Louise. He left word with a servant that he would be riding in Hyde Park for the next hour or so, and would return to Mlle. de Merivange after that.

Cleo was awake when Charles entered her boudoir, but she chose to remain alone, so did not acknowledge his presence. After he had left, she rang for her morning tea and set about planning her day. She would take her carriage into the park later, certainly. Her infatuation with Charles had kept her too long from display. Besides, she had enjoyed her encounter with Trevenaugh last night, and sensed in his stiffness and general aloofness a resistance which, she thought, indicated the presence of a spark of their affair which might be rekindled into another, much more intense flame—particularly now that he was a duke and had access to considerably more wealth than in the past. It had been just that lack of means that had caused Cleo to break off the affair she had conducted with Trevenaugh almost two years before. He had been ardent, persuasive, malleable—but, ultimately, rather poor. She had regretted the necessity of dismissing him—but then, she had to live. Now, of course, Trevenaugh would have no such problems. Of course, she would have to do something about Charles—very likely send him packing. She would miss him, but, with Trevenaugh as a replacement, not too much. She resolved to turn her attention to the matter.

And there was the business with Castleton. She frowned at the thought of it. A visitor . . . an *important* visitor who would come to her. . . . She shrugged and decided she would worry about that gentleman when the time came.

There was a knock on the door, and a servant entered. "Lord Castleton is below, ma'am, and wishes to see you," she said.

Cleo made a little moue of displeasure, and briefly flirted with the idea of turning him away. Then she thought better of it, and directed that he be sent up.

Castleton entered with his usual equanimity, but there was something different in his behavior that alerted Cleo. She could not at first divine the cause of his strangeness; then with a flash she recognized the symptoms she had seen before: Castleton was after something. The signs were slight, but unmistakable to one who knew him as well as she did—a controlled fidgeting, a contained sharpness, a roving eye that was constantly being checked, and an all-but-imperceptible air of distraction. Cleo wondered what it was that he wanted, and decided that if it was something from her he would either work very hard or pay very high to get it.

"My dear Castleton! What a pleasure to find you in my chamber so early in the day. It's like a royal levy to arise in such company."

"It is not so very early. I have been abroad for several hours," he said snappishly.

"Ah well, you young bucks are so hardy. Not even a reception at Josie van Scuyden's can deck you. As it did me. I found it tedious—aside from your own charming company, of course."

As though he had not heard her, Castleton said, "I did not expect to find you alone, Cleo. Has your young friend already decamped?"

"Charlie? Is it Charlie you are looking for?" asked Cleo, surprised. "He has gone to ride in the park, I believe, but will return shortly. Why do you wish to see him?"

"Why, we have business to discuss," said Castleton dryly.

Cleo laughed. "Surely you are not going to demand payment from him?"

Castleton looked at her solemnly. "Indeed I am. That is precisely what I'm going to do."

"But Castleton, whatever for? It's such a paltry sum for you," Cleo asked with genuine curiosity.

"The sum is unimportant. Principle is involved."

"But I know that he has not the money. What are you going to do? Have him put in the Fleet?"

"Perhaps it will not be necessary, my dear Cleo. The Englestons have something else that can be bartered for the debt."

"What is this game you're playing, Castleton?" asked Cleo, relishing the situation.

He paused a long moment, looking over her shoulder at nothing at all. Then he said, "It is time I married."

Cleo found the statement surprising. She

looked at Castleton with widened eyes. "But what ever for, and why now? And who? And what does Charlie have to do with this affair?"

Castleton looked annoyed at the string of questions, and for a moment it seemed as though he would answer none of them. Then with a sigh he replied, "I am going to marry because it is fitting that a man in my position have a wife and children. I am in my prime. It is time I propagated myself. I have met a suitable young lady who, as circumstances would have it, is exactly right for my purposes. She is the perfect beginning of a wife.—After I have smoothed out some of the details, she will be the envy of my peers. As for 'Charlie,'" (he spoke the name with distaste) "he fits into my plan very closely—for the young lady in question is his sister."

Cleo was silent for a few minutes, absorbing this information. "And you are here to ask Charlie for his sister's hand?" she asked ironically.

"No, my dear, I am here to inform him of my intentions. There will be no request made."

"And the lady? Is she agreeable to this arrangement?"

"She is very young," Castleton snapped. "She *will* be agreeable, once she fully understands her good fortune." His mouth closed tightly and his jaw became firm.

"I take it, though, that at the moment her vision is somewhat clouded?" asked Cleo sweetly.

"She will come around," said Castleton. He looked at her with rancor, noting her smirk.

"And when she comes around, you are going to take her in hand and make of her the perfect wife?"

Castleton was annoyed at Cleo's manner. "This will not be my first experience in creating what a too-careless nature has failed to provide, you know. If you remember, when I needed a strumpet I was able to pluck one from the most unlikely setting and fabricate a passable specimen . . . although, granted, as a strumpet you had a better start than Miss Engleston has as a wife."

Cleo ceased to smile. "Then why have you chosen this woman?"

"Because she is young, hence malleable. She is beautiful. But most of all, she is obtainable on my terms."

"How so?" asked Cleo.

"My dear Cleo, what an inquisitive little pussycat you are today. I wonder why I indulge you so by answering your questions."

"You indulge me, Castleton, because you know that I might be of help," said Cleo tartly. "Now, how is it that this girl is available on your terms?"

"Her father owes me money—never mind for what, at the moment—and her brother has foolishly lavished that money on . . . another lady. I know these people. They spend all their time blathering about good name and honor. They are preoccupied with their reputations. Once the elder Engleston hears that his obligation has not been met—indeed, he might already know—he will come groveling to me and give me anything I ask. It is to his advantage, believe me, to stay on my good side. I shall demand the hand of his daughter, dowry-free, mind you, and he shall consider himself the most fortunate man alive." He paused and smiled at Cleo. "It is people like the Englestons, my dear Cleo, that give people like you and me such power in the world."

This idea brought a smile to Cleo's lips. "My power," she said, with a sweeping gesture over her body, "comes from a quite different source from yours, Castleton."

He shook his head very slightly. "You misunderstand the difference between resources, which is what you are vaunting now, and power, which is what I have. And it is because you lack in understanding that I am so valuable to you. Remember that."

They looked at each other with carefully disguised hostility and distaste. Cleo pursed her lips and shrugged. "So, what do you plan? Where is this paragon of a future wife? How did you flush her from her country lair?"

"I discovered her at Carlton House last night, hovering under the wing of the Duchess of Bledrough."

Cleo sat up. "Why, that is Trevenaugh's aunt. Is he involved in this affair?"

"I don't know yet just what the connection is. That is one of the things I wish to find out from your young friend."

"Charlie has not mentioned that he knows either the duchess or Trevenaugh . . . although last night they did exchange some remarks . . . but then Charlie asked me who Henry was. . . ." She was puzzled, and this put her in a bad mood. "I wonder if Charlie's been hiding things from me. I don't like that."

There was a knock on the door and Charles stepped into the room, flushed from his ride, his hair tousled and clothes carelessly disarranged. On his face there was a look of joyful anticipation that disappeared instantly when he saw Castleton, and was replaced by wariness.

"Charlie," said Cleo. "Did you enjoy your ride?"

"Very much, thank you," he replied, looking at Castleton.

Cleo watched them both. "This is a friend of mine, Charlie, Lord Castleton. I've mentioned him to you, I believe."

"Sir," said Charles.

Castleton nodded. He did not stand or in

any other way acknowledge the introduction, and his manner was as unconcerned as if he were completely alone in the room. Charles regarded him with growing hostility mingled with embarrassment. He looked at Cleo with a question in his eyes, which she chose to ignore. Instead she smiled and patted the bed beside her.

"Come sit, Charlie, and tell me who was in the park."

He crossed to her and sat down, still watching Castleton from the corner of his eye. "There was a great press, but I didn't recognize anybody," he said.

"Come, come. Surely you saw some of the *ton* there. It is the season, after all. You must be more observant, or I shall have to find another courier." She spoke with calculated playfulness.

"You know I can't recognize any of the *ton*, Cleo," he said sullenly. "I am not accustomed to London notables."

"Modest Charlie," exclaimed Cleo. "Word has come to me that you are much better connected than I had thought. Now tell me," she continued spitefully, "was the Duchess of Bledrough there by any chance?"

Charles started and turned widened eyes to her. "How did you come by that name?" he asked.

"Why, I heard that your two families were very close. In fact I hear that the duchess has a visitor now who is well known to you."

Charles had felt so guilty for the past three months that almost any incident could make him look culpable. He reacted to Cleo's question as though he had been caught at something shameful. He was blushing fiercely, and looked at her only a second before lowering his eyes. Then he glanced covertly at Castleton. His behavior confirmed both Castleton's and Cleo's suspicions that something interesting was being hidden from them.

"I just heard myself, last night, that Louise, my sister, was in London," said Charles shamefacedly. "She is staying with the duchess. I have no idea why."

Cleo's face was suffused with mock astonishment. "No idea why? Maybe your sister simply chose the duchess's house at random?"

Charles was taken aback at the spitefulness of her remark. He looked at her miserably. "Last night when I spoke to your friend, Trevenaugh, he said that it was an accident. . . ."

A pregnant silence greeted this remark. Charles looked pleadingly at Cleo, who returned his look with a cold and skeptical glance.

"Charlie, I fear you are not being open with me," she said. "I have gone to some pains to extricate you from your difficulties. I have put in a word for you in . . ." She glanced meaningfully at Castleton. "In certain quarters. And you are repaying me with deceit."

"Cleo, I swear I do not know anything of this matter. Louise came to London to . . . look for me. My father . . . I suppose . . . is worried. . . ." Charles was too embarrassed to continue. "We can talk about it when we are alone," he said in a low voice.

"There is no reason to wait," said Castleton. His voice startled both Cleo and Charles, and made the latter look apprehensive. "I believe I can safely say that all of us are interested in your circumstances." Castleton's mirthless smile and chilly stare made Charles's stomach clutch.

"You know who I am, I believe," Castleton continued, looking coldly at Charles.

"I know, sir, that you are the man to whom I was to discharge a debt," said Charles, trying to mask his shame with bravado and to keep a tremble from his voice. "And I know that I have betrayed that trust. But I shall, in some manner, repay you, sir. I do not know how, at the moment, but I shall do so as soon as is humanly possible."

"Very interesting sentiment," said Castleton. "How do you propose to effect this so laudable undertaking?"

"As I said, sir, I do not know at the moment," Charles replied stiffly.

"Suppose I suggest what will happen," said Castleton with a smile.

Hope leaped into Charles's eyes, and he cautiously raised his head. "Sir?" he said.

Castleton's smile disappeared. "You will never be able to pay me the money that is rightfully mine. You will protest and talk and whine and find excuses, but you will not pay me my money."

Charles looked as though he had been slapped. He had been clutching at an escape which, he thought, was going to be offered by Castleton. Instead he had been made more acutely aware of his predicament. He felt as though he had been dropped from a cliff. He blustered. "I assure you, sir, that I shall have this sum in your hands—"

Castleton sneered, "You *assure* me. You are in no position to assure me. I do not want your assurances. I want my money. I wanted it three months ago, when it was due."

Charles was painfully aware of Cleo's watching them. "You have no right to talk to me this way. Take care you do not go too far."

Castleton rolled his eyes to the ceiling, then focused them on Charles. "You do not seem to understand that you are not in a position to discuss rights. If I choose, I could have you put into the Fleet at this moment. All I have to do is clap my hands and you will be carried off to rot until the money is repaid. Do not tempt me by babbling of what I have a right to do."

Charles was more frightened now, and the weight of his shame at being humiliated in front of Cleo was enough to crush him. He started to speak, but then lapsed into silence.

After a minute Castleton said, "Perhaps your friend, the Duchess of Bledrough, will lend you the money?" He was still curious about the relationship, and wished to know the origin and strength of it.

"I have never even seen the Duchess of Bledrough," said Charles miserably. "I do not know how my sister came under her protection, but I know that I will not benefit by the friendship, if that is what it is."

"Well, then," said Castleton after a pause. "What's to be done?"

He glanced mildly around the room, a little smile lingering on his lips. His eyes rested again on Charles, who had remained silently sitting at the foot of Cleo's silver barque.

Castleton cleared his throat. "As it happens, I am kindly disposed toward you and your family. This is fortunate for you, under the circumstances," he added drily.

Still Charles did not respond, but there was an air of anticipatory silence in the room.

Castleton continued. "I have known your father for many years. Quite recently—very recently, in fact—I made the acquaintance of your sister. And now I meet you." He paused. "That is the whole family, I believe?"

"It is, sir," said Charles in a low voice. He was lulled by Castleton's manner, and once more was fired by the thought that a solution to his predicament was imminent. He watched Castleton carefully and hopefully.

"Yes. In fact, I had quite an interesting discussion with your sister just this morning. We have come to an understanding."

"I don't follow you, sir," said Charles carefully.

"What I am saying is that I intend to make your sister my wife."

Charles did not know what he felt, at this news. He had been so battered during the last half hour that he had very little feeling left, except curiosity.

"I was not aware that you knew Louise so well as that—"

"As I said, I have known her but a short time. A short but sufficient time."

"Well. That is surprising news . . . indeed . . . all the more so because Louise is not an impulsive person—"

"That is good news. I am suspicious of impulsiveness."

"But I don't understand. How long have you known her? . . . Where did you meet?"

Castleton was annoyed at the questions and

would have ignored them. Cleo, however, was relishing the scene and spitefully piped up. "He met her just yesterday at Carlton House, Charlie," she said with mock rapture. "It was love at first sight—" Castleton flashed her a look of such balefulness that she lapsed into silence.

Charles did not see the look that passed between them, for he was too stunned by Cleo's information. "Just yesterday!" he exclaimed. "But I—you can't mean that you have already planned to be married after meeting just yesterday."

"Yes," said Castleton, "that is precisely what I have been saying, and hence what I mean."

"That does not sound like the sort of behavior Louise is capable of," said Charles, who was becoming more confused and uneasy. "Are you sure you have understood her?"

"I am not deficient in understanding," said Castleton, coldly.

"I am sure not, sir. Forgive me. I am so surprised."

Charles's rapid acquiescence softened Castleton somewhat, and he added, "Actually, Miss Engleston is not entirely and completely persuaded of the advantage of our union. This will come in time, however."

"Then you have not decided upon marriage, really, as of yet."

"On the contrary," said Castleton testily. "I *have* decided. We shall be married, and shortly."

"But it sounds as though you were trying to coerce my sister. . . . There is something very strange here."

Castleton was exasperated at being questioned by a young man of no particular distinction who was half his age. He snapped, "There is nothing for you to understand. You have no say in the matter. Your only contribution to my forthcoming marriage is a bad debt. I have heard enough of your questions."

Charles was startled, then wary. "Then I am right. You are trying to force my sister . . . or something similar . . . or . . ." Then a realization struck him and he went pale. "You are using my default to marry Louise," he said, slowly and with repugnance, directed as much toward himself as Castleton. "You have taken advantage of my bad debt to try to force a marriage on Louise," he said, becoming more indignant as he spoke. "You are forcing Louise to marry you in order that I may stay out of debtor's prison." He was standing, and looking defiantly at Castleton. "You have mistaken your adversary. I would rather languish for the rest of my days in the darkest hole in England before becoming party to such a scheme. I shall not permit my sister to marry you. You are a scoundrel. Call the warders! Send me to prison! You might as well be done with it quickly, for I shall never allow you to see my sister again."

Castleton remained seated, and regarded Charles with a cold distaste. "You are a fool," he said. "Your unpaid debt, paltry as it is, will serve me no other purpose than to furnish means of being rid of you if I should find that convenient. And I well might. You are presumptuous to think it could possibly be of greater consequence. With or without your debt, I shall have your sister as my wife—because I choose to do so. That is all."

"We shall see about that!" said Charles, his eyes blazing. "When I heard my sister was in London, I was too ashamed to go to her. Now that I have heard what has happened, I should be ashamed if I did not go immediately. I am going to her now, and am taking her back to Twelve Elms, away from you and your threat of marriage."

"You are doing nothing of the sort. You are going to do exactly what I tell you to do," said Castleton very calmly, his face a mask of satisfaction.

"You are insane to make such an assumption."

"I am quite sane. I am also, as far as you and your family are concerned, the most powerful person on earth. I own your family."

"You go too far. Say no more or I shall demand satisfaction. You have pressed the limits already."

Castleton laughed. "You have no idea what the limits are, you posturing fool." He spoke with such certainty that Charles was halted in his departure. "I can do with you what I will—and, mercifully, for you, I choose to marry your sister. There are thousands of other possibilities."

"You are talking nonsense," said Charles, but with shaken confidence. The indignation that had carried him to such moral heights a few moments before was quickly dissipating under the glacially calm pronouncements from Castleton.

"I had hoped," continued Castleton, "that it would not be necessary to disclose the source of my power over your family. But you leave me no choice."

Both Cleo and Charles were watching Castleton with fascination. He seemed impervious to their stares and continued talking as though he were entertaining an acquaintance with an anecdote about some stranger.

"I can do what I will because, if I choose, I can have your father swinging from a gallows within a fortnight." There was a gasp from Charles. "You see," continued Castleton, "your father is a smuggler and a murderer, and I have the proof."

Chapter 9

When Louise left the drawing room to fetch her bonnet and shawl in order to accompany the duchess on another foray against the London shops, Trevenaugh had been ostentatiously examining an urn with meticulous attention—even though he must have seen it hundreds of times. He continued his examination now that he was alone with the duchess, giving her the opportunity to inspect him with some shrewdness. After a silence of several minutes, during which Trevenaugh held the urn aloft in order to better see its base, the duchess said,

"How did they strike you together?"

Trevenaugh turned composedly toward her with a quizzical glance, and said, "Ma'am?"

"How did it seem to you our guest was faring with Lord Castleton? You saw them together, did you not?"

Trevenaugh replaced the urn and carefully centered it on its pedestal before replying nonchalantly, "I did not really notice. He left shortly after I arrived."

"Mmmm," said the duchess. Then, "Was their parting a promising one?"

"I don't follow you, ma'am."

"Did it look as though he would return soon?"

"I believe something was said about another visit—though I didn't mark it particularly. But, yes, I think something was mentioned about his calling again."

"And what was her attitude toward him?"

"She was respectful."

"How do you mean?"

"She listened and spoke little."

"Really, Henry, you are being very close about the matter. What was he saying that she was listening to?"

"I do not recall. Compliments, very likely."

With a sigh of exasperation, the duchess settled into one of the little gilt chairs and regarded Trevenaugh. He was staring out of the window into the garden, seemingly unaware of the scrutiny.

"She is very pretty, don't you think?" said the duchess.

"Ma'am?"

"Our visitor, Miss Engleston, is a very pretty girl, wouldn't you say?"

"Yes, she is attractive."

"It's a pity she doesn't have a fortune to go with her looks, or I might be able to create a brilliant future for her. As it is, however, we are already on the start toward a perfectly respectable one—more than that, actually, if she does indeed snare Castleton."

Trevenaugh said nothing.

The duchess continued, "For a brief while last evening I thought that you showed a certain interest in her."

"Me? Not at all," said Trevenaugh, with no particular emphasis.

"Oh, I know that it would be only a passing interest if it existed at all. Her beauty is too strongly defined for the Trevenaugh taste."

For the first time during their conversation, Trevenaugh regarded the duchess with something like interest.

"I find that a most peculiar statement, ma'am."

"That's because you have not had the opportunity to observe several generations of Trevenaughs, my dear Henry. Your ancestors—and doubtless, you, also, in time, will do the same—have shown a marked penchant for plain women. Some of them, it is true, have had certain redeeming qualities. Your great-great-grandmother Charlotte, for example, reputedly had the most luxuriant hair and eyebrows in the kingdom. . . . Although I suspect these features were singled out because it was impossible to find any thing else about her appearance that was commendable.

Her portrait is in the gallery at Wickenshire—she is quite hideous, really."

Trevenaugh regarded the duchess coolly. "I can assure you, ma'am, that I have an adequately developed sense of female beauty."

"Of course you do. So did your ancestors. They simply chose to marry plain women. I can't imagine why. I don't think it was a criterion they imposed on their spouses. It just happened. On the other hand, they have always bred very handsome progeny—witness you and me, for example. . . ." the duchess made an only partially mocking gesture at the both of them.

"Be that as it may, ma'am, I can assure you that I have no intention of searching out a homely woman as my wife. In fact, I have no intention of searching out a wife."

"That's good news, Henry. Miss Engleston wouldn't do for you. You are drifting now, and need someone of very strong character to take you in hand. Miss Engleston would not serve that purpose."

Trevenaugh regarded the duchess with irritation. "I think that you misread my character to make such an observation. I cannot imagine how you arrived at it."

"Years of experience, my dear boy. Trust your aunt. She knows what's best for you."

Trevenaugh seemed dubious, but said nothing.

"Furthermore," the duchess continued, after a pause, "most of the Trevenaughs have married women of very exalted families. Homely, perhaps, but of impeccable breeding. I'm afraid that Miss Engleston doesn't satisfy that requirement either—although she is, I am sure, quite respectable."

"My dear aunt, you seem to have imagined a relationship that does not exist," Trevenaugh said. "I have no interest whatsoever in Miss Engleston as a prospective bride—nor in any other capacity, for that matter." He turned again toward the window and clasped his hands behind his back.

"That's good news, my dear boy. I'm delighted to hear it. For a brief while I was afraid you were showing an unexpected streak of originality. That is the last thing in the world I should like to see in a Trevenaugh male."

Trevenaugh sighed with exasperation, but was prevented from answering by the return of Louise, who entered adjusting her shawl. She sensed uneasiness, and looked from the duchess to Trevenaugh, who remained with his back to the room. The duchess smiled ingenuously and said:

"So we are ready to go now. Henry, we shall leave you to your own devices. We had best be off."

Louise had composed herself after her encounter with Castleton, but she had not been able to erase her embarrassment at being misunderstood by Trevenaugh. She was, without knowing why, ashamed and guilty, as though she had done something reprehensible. She wanted Trevenaugh's approbation, but he would not even look at her. Above all, she wanted him to understand that Castleton meant nothing to her except a threat against her father—but his manner was so unbreachably cold that she could not mention the subject, much less advance an explanation.

She was longing to ask his aid. She was so alone and without defenses—for the duchess would not be of any help in the matter. All these feelings were going through her mind as she had prepared to go out again, and now that she was so close to Trevenaugh, but unable to even talk to him, she felt frustrated and helpless.

She was not eager to go on another expedition. It struck her as being a hollow and wasteful pastime, for she was more than ever convinced that she must leave London as soon as possible, and leave all her newly acquired finery behind her. She had been, she realized, little more than a toy for the duchess—something to dress up and animate and parade in society (much the same way, evidently, that Charles had been another type of toy for Cleo de Merivange) and she was angry and disgusted at having been so used. Yet none of this showed on her surface, for politeness had been bred into her, and she was aware that any sign of ingratitude or restiveness on her part would have been ill bred. So she adjusted her shawl and smiled quietly in reply to the duchess's remark.

If the duchess suspected Louise's true feeling she did not show it, for she set about preparing for their departure with her usual air of good-natured brightness. She summoned servants and gave orders and chattered vivaciously between times with both Trevenaugh and Louise.

The latter sat quietly, and surreptitiously watched Trevenaugh, who had returned to his inspection of the urn. Once she caught him looking at her, but his eyes escaped locking with hers in an instant, and he seemed careful to avoid any similar encounters.

". . . and if the Countess of Tewkenberry calls, tell her that I am out of town," said the duchess to the footman. Then she turned to Louise and Trevenaugh and added, "She will see me tonight at the Marlborough reception, of course, and know perfectly well that I am right here, but that will have made my point all the more clearly. . . ." She told the footman to summon her cook, and, when he arrived, launched a discourse on fresh strawberries. A footman entered and announced:

"There is a Mr. Charles Engleston here, Your Grace."

Louise rose to her feet with a gasp, and the duchess stared. Trevenaugh replaced the urn and turned toward the door. All three were silent for long enough to disconcert the footman, who grew red under their combined scrutiny. Then simultaneously Louise said, "Oh, Charles . . ." and the duchess said, "You may show him in." In the next instant Charles stood before them, looking breathless, disheveled, haughty, confused, and relieved.

"Hello, Louise," he said.

In an instant she rushed to him and threw her arms about his neck. He stood stiffly and awkwardly, allowing her to embrace him. He glanced surreptitiously at Trevenaugh and the duchess.

"Oh, Charles, I'm so happy to see you," said Louise, close to tears. "So much has happened and I have so much to tell you, to ask you—"

"We are *all* happy to see you," said the duchess imperiously. "We have been very worried about you," she added with an admirably feigned sincerity. Then, with a severity tempered by good humor, she said, "You have caused this dear child a great deal of sorrow."

"I was not aware that she was in London, ma'am," said Charles with conventional contriteness, all the while disengaging himself from Louise's embrace. "I am truly sorry for the pain I have caused you," he said to her.

"Charles. I've forgotten it already, now that I've found you and see that you are unharmed. I'm so glad that all is well and that we can go back to Twelve Elms now."

Confusion and distress crossed his face, and he hesitated before speaking. "We can't leave . . . right away, at least. . . . I'm afraid that it will be impossible to go back as soon as you would like. . . ." He drew his hand distractedly across his forehead and looked questioningly around the room, as though he were seeking a solution to some deep problem on the exquisitely painted walls.

The duchess misunderstood his hesitation and said, in a chiding tone, "Surely you can terminate a liaison that has caused so much pain to your dear sister?" At Charles's look of surprise and confusion, the duchess continued, "Oh yes, we know all about your connection to a certain person, but now you must put that behind you. You must turn away from a situation which can lead only to unhappiness for your family." The duchess was so enjoying her evangelical role that she failed to notice the hostile cloud that was settling over Charles's face.

"That liaison—as you call it—is none of your affair," Charles said coldly.

The duchess was stunned into silence, followed shortly by outrage. It had been decades since she had been spoken to sharply. She was unaccustomed to even a hint of opposition, and she certainly did not expect to find it in her own drawing room, coming from some country upstart. She drew herself up and her eyes flashed. She had opened her mouth to speak when Louise intervened.

"Oh, please excuse him, ma'am. He would never have been so rude if he had known of the kindness you have shown me."

Charles appeared to be already regretting his words, and was looking sheepish—though his attitude remained tinged with huffiness. The duchess was not calmed and seemed to be preparing a verbal assault when all three of them were startled by Trevenaugh, silent until then, who said:

"I'm sure the young man regrets his hastiness. I can well imagine the strain he's under."

"Thank you, sir," said Louise, looking at Trevenaugh with admiration. He returned her look with what seemed to her like a hint of warmth.

Finally Charles said to the duchess, "Please forgive me, ma'am. I spoke too quickly. I have just learned some very disturbing news and am laboring under the burden of it."

The duchess was somewhat mollified by the apologies, but was by no means ready to forgive out of hand the first harsh words she had heard in several years. She bowed, distantly, coldly, and regally—and sailed from the room without a word.

Her departure constrained the remaining three, particularly Trevenaugh, who seemed to have been forced into a position of unexpected intimacy with the other two. For the first time since she had met him, Louise saw uneasiness, and remarked that even in such a position he manifested discomfort more elegantly than she had thought possible. Charles, also, seemed embarrassed, whether because he felt responsible for having precipitated the departure of the duchess, or for some other reason, she could not tell.

She felt calm. She had come to London to find Charles, and here he was. For the moment she forgot about Lord Castleton and his threats, both of matrimony and harm to her father. She basked in the first comfort she had felt in two days—that of knowing she had accomplished what she had set out to do. Then she looked at Trevenaugh, who was standing aloofly to one side, preparing to leave, and felt a pang—for she thought that now she would have to forgo the possibility of ever breaking through his exterior. Though she had never really expected to come to know him well, she had hoped to gain his esteem—or at the very least his attention.

Charles said, "Louise, Lord Castleton is a blackguard and a scoundrel. He has the power to . . . harm . . . father. He says he is going to use it unless you marry him." He looked desperate and angry.

"I know," said Louise. "I wanted so much to ask you what to do. He was here this

morning. . . . He is a frightening . . . a
loathsome man."

Trevenaugh, who had been starting toward
the door, stopped as though struck, and
turned sharply to Louise. She looked at him
hesitantly and blushed. With her eyes lowered she said:

"I realized that you had misunderstood the
object of my meeting with Lord Castleton
this morning. I did not know how to correct
the impression—"

"But," said Trevenaugh, concern showing
through his veneer, "why didn't you tell me
that this man was threatening you? I would
have had him thrown out and beaten."

"I couldn't—I—" began Louise.

"But why not?" said Trevenaugh. Distress
brought a sharp edge to his manner, making
his request more imperious than, perhaps, he
would have wished.

"Because, sir, nothing in your demeanor
invited me to make such confidences." Louise
spoke with exasperation and pent-up anger,
thinking back to that morning, when she
would have almost gone on her knees to get a
kind or concerned word from Trevenaugh.

He was silent with surprise and consternation, and seemed to be considering her remark. He walked to the window and looked
out, his forehead creased with thought.

Charles had paid little attention to their
exchange, being absorbed in his own role in

the affair. As though the other two had not spoken, he said, "It's all my fault. If only I had not met . . . if only I had not spent the money I was to give Castleton . . . It's I who am guilty of putting you in this position, Louise. I beg your forgiveness." He spoke melodramatically, but his remorse was sincere.

Both Louise and Trevenaugh turned toward him, surprised.

It was Louise who asked, "Why did you have money for Lord Castleton?"

"Father sent it to him. . . . That was my commission—to deliver a sum of money into the hands of Lord Castleton and return to Twelve Elms—and I failed." Charles threw himself on one of the little gilt chairs and put his head in his hands. In spite of her sympathy for his suffering, Louise could see that he could not help introducing histrionics into his announcement. She went to him and put her hand on his shoulder.

Trevenaugh asked Louise, "What is the threat that Castleton holds over your father?"

"He didn't tell me . . . exactly. . . . He only said that he could have him . . . hanged." She shuddered and turned toward Charles.

"That is nonsense," said Trevenaugh. "He is blustering, making idle threats, taking advantage of a young girl's natural fear—"

"It is not nonsense!" exclaimed Charles.

"He has proof that father is a smuggler . . . and a murderer."

Louise grew pale and, if Trevenaugh had not rushed to her side, might have fallen. He helped her into a chair. Then he said:

"You have seen this proof?"

"No, I have not seen it," said Charles miserably, "but Castleton says he has it . . . and I believe him."

"What is it?" Trevenaugh asked.

"It's a signed confession from father, giving all the details of a night that happened over twenty-five years ago, telling how during a smuggling trip from France he met a patrol of revenue officers and during a skirmish he killed one of them. It's a signed document. Castleton says it is incontrovertible proof of father's guilt. He spoke in such a way as to convince me he was not lying."

After a moment's silence Trevenaugh turned to Louise. "Can you believe what Castleton says about your father?"

"Never," said Louise. "Father is gentleness and kindness personified. I have never heard a violent word from him. I cannot imagine—"

"Louise," Charles interrupted, "we really don't know father very well." He spoke matter-of-factly.

Louise looked at him for a long moment, then she said, "I cannot—will not—believe that father is capable of murder."

Charles shrugged. He looked very unhappy.

Trevenaugh asked, "Was this the first time that your father has ever sent money to Castleton?"

"I don't know," he said miserably, "but I don't think so. He has made a trip to London every year for as long as I can remember, and at about the same time I came this year."

"What did Castleton say about the money to you?"

Charles blushed scarlet and lowered his head. "He said he wanted it, that my father owed it to him."

"Charles," Louise asked softly and unhappily, "what happened to the money?"

Instantly Charles became surly. He rose from the chair and walked away. For a moment it appeared he would leave. Then, he said, without facing them, "I spent it on a bracelet."

Trevenaugh seemed to sympathize with Charles as he said, "There is nothing we can do about that now. What is important to learn is why your father is sending money to Castleton. Did it have something to do with this 'proof' he says he has? Was your father paying Castleton to suppress the proof?"

"I don't know," said Charles. "Father told me nothing, and Castleton only told me what

I've told you. I don't know what the money was for."

"What we must do, then," said Trevenaugh decisively, "is to put our hands on this proof and destroy it."

Louise stared at Trevenaugh with surprise and hope.

"Do you think we can?" Charles asked doubtfully.

"We must," said Trevenaugh, as though he already had the situation well in hand. "Castleton is playing some game, apparently, and has been doing so for many years. When a man is engaged in such activity he leaves traces, creates confederates, causes talk. A little stirring up on our part will be sufficient to bring a great deal to light, I should think."

Louise could scarcely believe that this was the same man who had seemed to look at her from a great distance, when he noticed her at all. It was as though his elegant body had been invaded by a most congenial spirit. Welcome as the change was, it was confusing, and left her wondering what was responsible. She wondered also at his complete acceptance of her father's innocence simply on the strength of an acquaintance with his children. She was too happy with the change, however, to spend much time in speculation.

"I shall set about making inquiries today," Trevenaugh continued, "and we shall see what can be uncovered. In the meantime you might be making a few queries of your own. There is probably no one in London who knows Castleton better than Cleo de Merivange."

Charles looked uneasy and embarrassed as he shot a glance at Louise. "I don't think that I can . . . I don't know . . ."

"Do not hesitate to use Cleo for information because of her delicate feelings," said Trevenaugh drily. "She would show no such scruples for you."

"I am not hesitating because of Mademoiselle de Merivange's feelings, but because of my own," said Charles hotly, drawing himself to his full height and looking truculent.

After a pause, Trevenaugh said, "I see."

Louise was both embarrassed and annoyed at Charles's sudden and, in her view misplaced gallantry. She went to stand by Trevenaugh's side and asked,

"Is there something I should do?"

"I can think of nothing for the moment," he replied, and smiled almost shyly at her.

Charles, as though he felt left out, was almost sulky as he said, "I will, of course, do anything else you think may be necessary."

"For the time being I can foresee nothing," said Trevenaugh kindly. Charles seemed about to say something more, then was silent.

The door opened and the duchess, splendidly dressed in peach muslin with a bonnet to match, entered briskly.

"My, what a solemn group you are," she said brightly. "One would think you had come to witness a hanging."

Her remark, though inadvertent, seemed too apt, and gave Louise a start. The two men also seemed to notice the unhappy appropriateness of the observation, and looked at her oddly. She did not seem to mind as she turned to Louise.

"Well, my dear, we must not let the return of a brother—long lost though he may have been—interfere with the more important things, such as our shopping. Are you ready?" And she turned to Charles. "You will excuse your sister from waiting on you immediately, I hope. You can become acquainted with my nephew meanwhile, and perhaps you will be good enough to join us for dinner here this evening?"

Louise marveled at the resilience of the duchess's *amour propre* which, only half an hour before, had been so wounded as to render her speechless—and now had recovered sufficiently not only to allow her to ignore the late unpleasantness, but to act as though it had never occurred.

Charles bowed his acquiescence.

After a small hesitation, Louise answered, "I shall be most happy to accompany you, ma'am. But there is, of course, no further need for me to own any more finery, since my stay in London will be over very quickly."

"A well-rounded wardrobe is an asset, even in the wilderness," said the duchess. "Besides, I must finish polishing you up and marrying you off. I loathe unfinished business. And Henry, perhaps you can do something with the young man," she added imperiously.

Charles stiffened and Louise feared another outburst, so she hastened to say, "We are both so grateful for all you have done for us, ma'am. Very soon we shall be returning to Twelve Elms, and then you shall be quit of the nuisance we have caused you."

"No nuisance at all, my dear. Every moment a pleasure. As I told you—was it only two days ago?—I am delighted that you have afforded me the opportunity to see things through fresh eyes. Such opportunities are rare, and I have been fortunate in having the power to seize them when they come my way. Shall we go?"

Trevenaugh said to Louise, "I shall meet you here at dinner, and let you know what I have been able to uncover."

The duchess raised her eyebrows. "More mystification? You have found the missing brother. What more is there to uncover?"

"It appears, ma'am, that Miss Engleston may have some further difficulties to smooth over before departing London."

"And what may they be?" said the duchess, her glance bright and interested.

"I shall leave that to Miss Engleston to disclose, if she chooses."

"Ah, good. She can tell me in the carriage. So, it appears, you will be with us a little longer, my dear. How delightful. We shall culminate your stay in a splendid marriage yet." And she swept from the room. After a glance at Trevenaugh and Charles, Louise followed her.

The two men, left alone, were uneasy. It was Trevenaugh who broke the silence.

"We shall be meeting here for dinner, then, I believe?"

"Indeed, sir, that seems to be the plan," said Charles.

"Until this evening then."

"Sir."

Solemnly they shook hands and each went his separate way.

Chapter 10

Nathan Brombedge was dying. He had known it for some time, though he had refused to allow the knowledge to govern his behavior. He pretended that nothing was wrong. But now, as pain clutched and tore at his entrails like some vicious beast, he writhed, and the pretense in the face of such brutal reality disappeared.

His involuntary spasm distracted Castleton, who was standing over him. "Stop fidgeting," he said testily, "and let us get on with this letter."

"Yes, m'lord," said Brombedge, after a pause that was sufficient to give him enough breath for an answer. He bent over the paper and repeated the last phrase he had written: "'. . . and to this purpose, my dear Louise, I shall address myself assiduously.'"

"Yes . . . very well, continue: 'On the other hand, if you should not see fit to couple your destiny with mine, I shall pursue the matter we discussed, relentlessly. This would prove painful to me, and no doubt to you and to one you hold dear. Let us act in such a way as to make this latter course unnecessary. I am, ma'am, your humble servant, et cetera, et cetera. . . .' Very well. That is to go to Miss Engleston this evening. Take it yourself. After delivering the letter, you will pass by Mademoiselle de Merivange and tell her I wish to meet with her later tonight . . . alone."

"Yes, m'lord," said Brombedge, expressionlessly. His face was white and covered with beads of perspiration.

"Then," continued Castleton, oblivious to his secretary's condition, "return to me with the time of the meeting. Now, was there anything else? . . ."

"I believe not, m'lord," said Brombedge quietly. The pain had subsided once more, and Brombedge was able to resume his ordinary manner.

"I shall go to the club now, where I shall be for the rest of the afternoon. I shall expect you here tonight with word from Mademoiselle de Merivange."

"Yes, m'lord," said Brombedge.

Castleton left the library without a backward glance.

For a few minutes Brombedge did not move, waiting fearfully for a new attack from his body. Then, little by little, he sensed an easing and a freedom, for the moment, from the most extreme pain. He stared at the letter he had just written, then folded and sealed it. Castleton hardly ever put his own signature to his letters. Brombedge smiled slightly as he thought of the caution that his master was employing, even in the wooing of a wife. His smile took on depth as he thought how useless this caution was to prove. For Nathan Brombedge was going to have his revenge—and very shortly.

He had been Castleton's secretary for more than a quarter of a century—though secretary was too finite a term, he reflected bitterly. *Serf* would be more apt. Serf, indeed, since he had had no life, no pleasure, had drawn no breath that was not immediately dependent upon Castleton's whim. He had made just one mistake and had spent a lifetime paying for it. The hatred that his bondage had inspired had been all the more intense for being subterranean. It had festered and grown—much the same way as the disease that was now eating away his life. And just as that disease had now erupted in unbearable pain, so his impotent hatred was going to erupt in one last superbly vengeful act.

He was not yet sure just what the act would be, but it was beginning to take shape in his mind. And, once perpetrated, it would mean the ruin of Castleton. It was the intensity of Brombedge's desire for revenge that kept him ambulatory. He had nothing else to live for.

In spite of his pain and rancor he set about putting Castleton's affairs in order—just as he had done every day for a quarter century. The dull routine which was so onerous was also his greatest comfort—it was what gave his life shape and substance. So he arranged letters, bills to be paid, reports from Castleton's properties, and systematically dispatched them. Then he took a strongbox from a concealed drawer in the desk, and searched out the key on his chain. There were only two keys to the box—his and Castleton's. He reflected that there had been one time in his life when he had been enormously proud of this fact. In such a way does the leashed and muzzled dog adore its master. He had been flattered because in this box was the only thing Castleton valued in the world—the source of his power. And by having access to it, it became, in a sense, his—Brombedge's—power also. There had been a time when he would thrill with a sense of omnipotence when he just handled the strongbox. Then pain and the awareness of an encroaching death had stripped the box of its fascination, and Brombedge had been wrenched into reality and seen it for what it was—the container of shabby and victimized, weak and ruined men. The wretched scraps of paper the box contained might as well have been so many rotting corpses—for, once they were consigned to the strongbox, the souls of their writers belonged to Castleton. And he, Brombedge, had been the keeper of those souls for many years, even though his own was among the lot. For he also had been—and still was—the victim of Castleton's lust for power. His own scrap of paper was in that strongbox—if not actually at present, at least symbolically. One youthful misstep had been sufficient to consign Brombedge to the life of a serf. He had accommodated himself to the situation—he had not, he reasoned, fallen from such great heights, after all—but now that he was watching his life dwindle and close in on him he raged at the visions of what might have been. The money he might have earned, the women he might have known, the family he might have raised, all danced with tantalizing deliciousness before his eyes. His hatred for the man who, he reasoned, had kept all these things from him grew in proportion to his pain and sense of mortality.

He had thought of destroying the contents of the strongbox—but that would not have really been satisfactory. So many of the men whose lives were shaped by the pieces of paper therein would not know that those scraps had ceased to exist, if Castleton chose not to tell them. So the power over their lives, the power in the hands of Castleton, would be just as great, at this point, whether the various documents existed or not. No, destruction was not the answer. Exposure was what was needed. But exposure to whom and in what manner? That was the problem Brombedge was wrestling with. Meanwhile, he continued to check the papers to see that the various commitments were being met, to see that the victims were still honoring their oppressor.

He shuffled through the documents, remarking late payment here, a lack of payment there, a cessation of communication . . . and duly noted everything on a list for the attention of Castleton. When he had finished, it was late in the day. He thought of trying to eat something, but the knowledge of what any kind of sustenance would do to his stomach made him break out in sweat.

He dressed carefully in his dark breeches and dark coat, with white shirt and cravat, fetched his worn but still presentable hat (a castoff from Castleton) and left the house with the letter for Miss Engleston. Out of habit he walked to economize, though he was weak from the onslaughts of pain and lack of nourishment. He was jostled several times by street urchins who sensed his weakness and took advantage of it. They jeered at him and asked for money, but he ignored them and continued inexorably on his way. He left the letter with the duchess's footman, and proceeded to the house of Cleo de Merivange.

He had to wait a few minutes below while he was being announced. Cleo was in her boudoir, he supposed. He wondered whether she would be alone, or whether young Charles Engleston would be with her—he smiled bitterly at the irony of that particular liaison.

Presently the footman invited him to ascend.

He entered the boudoir, as always, quietly and diffidently, his eyes lowered, his manner humble and circumspect. He took in, however, every detail. He was surprised to see one of Cleo's former lovers sitting elegantly at his ease in the far corner of the room. It was a moment or so before he remembered the name—Henry Trevenaugh, Duke of Wickenshire. Then with an inward start he remembered that the duke was the nephew of the duchess of Bledrough, with whom Louise Engleston was staying. Habit bred by a lifetime of intrigue made him try to piece this puzzle together. All the while he was looking demurely at the floor.

"Well, Brombedge, what is it?" asked Cleo impatiently.

"I have a message from his lordship," said Brombedge, softly enough to keep the man in the corner from hearing.

"Well, what is it?" said Cleo, making no effort to lower her voice. It was strident with impatience.

"His lordship wishes to know what hour

would be convenient." Brombedge was almost whispering.

"Oh fie. Tonight may well be impossible," said Cleo, somewhat more guardedly but with annoyance. "I might be . . . engaged." Involuntarily she glanced at the man in the corner.

"It is very important, ma'am," said Brombedge softly. "His lordship was most insistent."

"His lordship can go to the devil," said Cleo spitefully. "He thinks he can snap his fingers and make me jump through a hoop." Her green eyes were narrowed and glistening with vexation. Her golden curls were loose and hanging down to her shoulders, and her peignoir was in provocative disarray.

"She is making a great effort for the gentleman," thought Brombedge, though nothing showed in his face. He said, "Perhaps after midnight, ma'am? Lord Castleton holds the meeting most dear."

"Oh, very well. Tell him to come after midnight." She had lowered her voice, but it was so tinged with exasperation that she seemed to hiss her agreement.

Brombedge bowed and, his eyes giving a last guarded sweep of the room, he quietly left.

● ● ●

Cleo turned back to Trevenaugh; the annoyance which had been creasing her forehead had smoothed away. She presented a picture of serene gaiety.

"Forgive this interruption, Henry," she said lightly, and smiled at him affectionately. She walked toward him, her filmy peignoir floating around her, giving the impression that it would evaporate upon the slightest encouragement.

Trevenaugh watched her now, as he had watched the whole transaction with Brombedge, with a noncommittal smile.

"It is I who should ask forgiveness, Cleo, for having imposed myself on you at such short notice."

"Ah, you have not . . . yet . . . *imposed yourself* on me, my dear Henry. At least, not in any way that I might notice." Her eyes sparkled and her lips were slightly parted as she settled on her chaise longue, lightly as a cloud.

Trevenaugh acknowledged the innuendo with a slightly raised eyebrow and a nod. He did not, however, follow through. Instead, he remarked, "That was a most interesting caller you just had. I seem to remember him from my previous visits here. He has something to do with Lord Castleton, I believe?"

"He is Castleton's secretary," said Cleo tersely.

"Ah, yes. Castleton, then, is still one of your favored visitors."

"I see him occasionally."

"An interesting man, Castleton. I have never really conversed with him. I am told he is well informed and able."

"He is certainly well informed," said Cleo with a mirthless laugh. Then, as though she thought she had revealed too much, she changed the subject. "But tell me about your stay in the wilderness. Are the Indian ladies to your liking?"

"I saw none. In what way is he well informed? Is he interested in government?"

"I am not privy to Lord Castleton's interests," she replied brusquely.

"I should have thought just the contrary, that no one could know him better than you."

Cleo's expression lost its studied gaiety and became guarded.

"Why this sudden interest in Castleton, my dear Henry?"

"It is not so sudden, and, for that matter, it is not really an interest—I was just curious about the man."

"I will satisfy your curiosity on any score of subjects if I can, but I fear I can be of no help to you as far as Castleton is concerned. I hardly know the man."

Trevenaugh realized that he had struck a wrong note at the beginning of his questions, and he cursed himself for his clumsiness. He knew that there was no way of extricating information from Cleo now that she had been put on guard. So, with an inaudible sigh, he took Cleo's hand in his and held it lightly.

"Let us drop the subject," he said softly. "There are so many other more important things to discuss...."

This was a tone and a manner to which Cleo could respond without effort, and she immediately fell into her former pose.

"Henry, it's so nice to have you back. I've missed you terribly." She lied with a touching sincerity that almost convinced Trevenaugh. He reflected how easy it would be to let himself fall under Cleo's spell again. Then he remembered how high a price—not just monetary—anyone under her spell had to pay: The humiliations, the jealousies, the frustrations to which he had been subjected were not worth it. So he squeezed her hand with convincing tenderness and gazed into her eyes.

"I hope I shall be seeing you often, now."

"As often as you like," she whispered, and put her free hand on his neck, bringing her face near his expectantly. Trevenaugh was very tempted. She was desirable. But he feared he would never be able to stop with just one kiss, that there would be no checking the passion she could inspire if he were to allow her to start.

He disengaged himself and held both of her hands as he rose to his feet.

"I will want to see you later, Cleo. When there is more time. When I can spend hours with you."

Cleo was startled at the interruption. She reclined in the chaise longue and smiled up at him. "Come soon, Henry," she said. She remained prone as he kissed both her hands lightly and quickly left the boudoir.

Once he was on the street again he shook himself as though he had been under a spell. She really is a Circe, he thought. He was distressed at how near he had come to resuming his former role—that of helpless and hopelessly enchained lover. He was also annoyed that he had been able to learn nothing from her.

He walked along the fashionable street, nodding from time to time to acquaintances, and wondered what to do. He wanted to help Miss Engleston. She appealed to him in a way no other woman had ever appealed to him—she was helpless. He had been exposed only to the ruthlessly efficient woman—such as Cleo on the one hand, and on the other the equally ruthless and terribly capable type such as his aunt Isabel, the Duchess of Bledrough. Each woman was a manifestation of the same quality, in spite of their differences in social level: Each knew what she wanted and set about to get it, regardless of the consequences. His aunt, he reflected, was certainly more honest about her methods, but no less determined.

Such women had made Trevenaugh wary. In defense he had developed an exterior that he wore like chain mail—an elegant manner that was correct and chilling to the point of discouraging any but the most hardy. And this had been his defeat, ultimately, because the more gentle women of his class had been repelled by his manner, but the bolder and more aggressive ones had risen to the challenge and attacked with gusto. Trevenaugh had never been able to understand his dilemma.

His meeting with Louise Engleston had disconcerted him. He was, for the first time, exposed for a long period to helplessness and trust—genuine helplessness and trust, not the type so artfully feigned by women he had known in society. Louise was honestly in need of help and comfort, and he felt a surge of unusual power when he realized that he was in a position to supply both.

So it had become, in a very short space of time, an obsession with him to clear up the matter of Louise's father, and to arrange the Engleston family's affairs in the most handsome way possible.

But how to do so was a thornier problem

than he had at first surmised. He was certain
that Castleton—like everyone else—had his
Achilles heel. He was not really a cynical
man, but he had been in society long enough
to realize that everyone is vulnerable. Particularly if one has a scheme under way—as apparently Castleton did. If only he could
fathom just what the scheme was. Why
would a man like Castleton concern himself
with the affairs of the Engleston family at
Twelve Elms? Of what earthly use could
such a family be to him? True, he now
wanted to marry the daughter, but his interest had apparently dated to a time before
Louise was even born.

He had hoped that he could trick Cleo into
revealing something about Castleton. He
vaguely knew that her connection with him
was a strong one, though he was not—hardly
anyone was—aware of the particulars. Cleo
had seemed to appear magically under Castleton's protection several years before, long
before Henry had entered society. She had
sprung up as magically as a mushroom. By the
time Trevenaugh had met her she had been
established as one of the most sought out of
the Fashionable Impures, and Castleton—
though hovering in the background—had re-
linquished his exclusive hold on her. During
Trevenaugh's liaison with Cleo, Castleton's
name had never even been mentioned—
though, he thought bitterly, God knows ev-

erybody else's had been at one time or another.

But he had been wrong. Cleo would not be tricked and probably would not be bought—he sensed some strong loyalty there that he was powerless against. Now, as he walked toward his aunt's house, he tried to think of other sources who might be helpful. The difficulty was that though Castleton was in society he did not seem to have established any close relations—there were no friends, no relatives, no mistresses who were closely linked to his name. He was a mystery.

Trevenaugh was so preoccupied that he scarcely noticed the commotion in the road ahead of him. Then, when he did become aware of a group of noisy street urchins yelling and jumping in a circle and surrounding something, he was not interested enough to give more than a cursory glance at the hullabaloo. Such occurrences were not rare, and Trevenaugh was never one to meddle with the hoi polloi. But as he came abreast of the scuffle he caught a familiar shape and color in the corner of his eye. He looked at the group of young hooligans, all ragged and filthy, their hair matted and their grimy faces alight with the joy of tormenting another being, and saw in their center the black-coated and curiously passive Brombedge.

He was standing, slightly slumped, looking

off into the distance as though it were some-one else who was being pummeled and pulled at.

"'Ere now, there's a noice gennlemun," yelled one of the little thugs, "give us this 'ere coat, why don' cher? You've got another t' home." He was suiting action to words by pulling at Brombedge's sleeve, and his cohorts were quick to join in. "Give us the coat and we'll let cher go," one of them yelled.

Brombedge tried to keep his balance, but the contrary tugs were too much for him and he fell to his knees, trying feebly—it seemed almost indifferently—to protect his head from the random fists that were buffeting him.

Trevenaugh rushed into the fray and with a few well placed kicks dispersed the howl-ing children—none was older than ten years or so. One of them, the leader apparently, made an effort to stand his ground, but was soon dissuaded by a cuff on the head. Tre-venaugh helped Brombedge to his feet and set about brushing his coat.

Brombedge looked at Trevenaugh curi-ously, and quite calmly.

"Thank you, sir," he said. "They were a nasty lot."

"Indeed they were. This sort of thing is becoming much too common these days," said Trevenaugh, with the assurance of one who is certain that such things will never happen to him. "Are you recovered? You seem very pale. Perhaps a brandy or a glass of port?"

At the thought of assaulting his stomach with spirits, Brombedge blanched and little beads of sweat appeared on his forehead. This led Trevenaugh to assume that he was indeed in great need of something to drink.

"I could not assume further on your kindness, sir," said Brombedge humbly, but with his habitual calm and guarded expression.

"On the contrary, my good man," said Trevenaugh. "In fact, I welcome this opportunity to have a . . . chat with you. I would consider it an honor if you would join me."

Brombedge, after a quarter century of devious service, scented the undercurrent in Trevenaugh's invitation. His instinct told him that very possibly this was the opportunity he was looking for. After a brief hesitation he accepted. With Brombedge leaning on Trevenaugh's arm, the two men made their way to a nearby tavern.

Chapter 11

It was a lovely day, so the duchess and Louise were using the open carriage. Louise had left Trevenaugh and Charles with some trepidation. Given Charles's propensity to take offense at the merest hint of a slight, and given Trevenaugh's determined aloofness and intractability, it seemed to Louise that the combination was a volatile one. But she had little time to brood over the matter, for the duchess was relentless in her pursuit of facts and details about the latest development under her roof. She was having a difficult time assimilating the idea that it was Lord Castleton who was pursuing Louise, rather than the other way around. This seemed to her—so she stated more than once—a highly improbable state of affairs. At one point, during Louise's narration of Lord Castleton's tenacity, the duchess could not contain herself and burst out with:

"But my dear, this makes no sense. Castleton is rich and of an excellent name. *You* have *nothing*."

The brutality of the remark caused Louise to pause with surprise. She wondered briefly whether it was an observation that someone who regarded her with amiability would be capable of making. This was not a thought she was permitted to elaborate, however, for the duchess, avid for the complete story, pressed on. And Louise finally held nothing back, though it was with some misgivings that she told the details of the threat that Castleton held over her family. She sensed that it was not information that the duchess would handle delicately.

"So," said the duchess at the end of the narrative, "your father is headed for the gibbet if you don't marry Castleton." She paused thoughtfully. "Well, my dear, there are certainly more difficult ways to save a father. You could, for example, be asked to dispense your favors without marriage. After all, it seems that Lord Castleton has the upper hand." She paused again, then asked, "And when is the wedding to take place? Has he set a date yet?" She asked in the most interested fashion, and so matter-of-factly that for a moment Louise was disoriented. She wondered whether she had interpreted the question correctly.

"Indeed, ma'am, there will be no wedding," she said timidly.

"Mmmmmm," said the duchess. "Does this mean, then, that your father is to be hung shortly?"

"No, ma'am, certainly not," said Louise with indignation, made the stronger by the fear that possibly her refusal of Castleton would mean just that.

"Well, then, I don't understand, my dear. Are you expecting Lord Castleton to undergo a change of heart?" There was a very lightly disguised sarcasm in the duchess's voice.

"That seems to be very unlikely, ma'am," said Louise softly.

"Then how do you propose to reconcile the two situations?" the duchess asked with a bright and lively interest, turning her animated and quizzical face toward Louise.

Much against her will, for she sensed with growing apprehension the duchess's animosity toward her, Louise answered,

"Mr. Trevenaugh has said that he will see to the matter."

"Henry?" said the duchess with surprise. "Henry is going to meddle with this affair? That astonishes me. What is it he thinks he can do?" The question was actually rhetorical, but Louise answered it anyway.

"He is going to find a way of retrieving the confession—or whatever signed piece of paper it is that Lord Castleton has."

"Is he now?" said the duchess with

strident good humor. "And how is he to go about this?"

"I do not know, ma'am. Mr. Trevenaugh told me no particulars. I do not think that he was very clear himself as to how it was to be accomplished."

"It will be very ingenious, no doubt," said the duchess drily. "Well, your visit has certainly enlivened our affairs, my dear."

"I hope not to the point of your regretting your kindness, ma'am," said Louise. She was distressed at the turn their relationship had taken. Though she had never felt really warmly toward the duchess, nor had she discerned any similar feelings toward herself, she had experienced gratitude as she had basked in the duchess's good will. This good will now seemed to be turning rancid, and Louise could not understand why. The duchess had become decidedly prickly.

"Nonsense, child," said the duchess. "You have not been the recipient of my kindness, but of my interest. I told you that when we first met, if you remember." She was speaking the truth. All her gestures were inspired by a fierce self-interest, a fact which she never disguised from herself and rarely tried to hide from others. What she did not say to Louise—though she felt it very strongly—was that now that the situation had gone beyond her control she no longer found it amusing. She did not like to play games in which other people made the rules, and it seemed to her that was what was happening now. She had taken a little girl from the country and put her under protection with the idea of transforming her. There was indeed a transformation afoot, but the duchess was no longer directing it. Hence it ceased to divert her. She was only waiting and watching for the opportunity to terminate the situation. In the meantime, however, she was making the best of contrary circumstances. So she played out the charade she had originally devised as though nothing had changed.

Louise did not know how to respond to the duchess's remark, so she said nothing.

The two women rode in silence for some minutes before arriving at their destination, still another shop.

As they descended, the duchess was chatting once more with a lively and animated air about the necessity of a complete wardrobe for a young woman. She appeared in splendid spirits. Louise followed her quietly.

But the exhilaration of the first days was missing, and even the duchess, who usually seemed capable of self-generating enthusiasms, seemed to become bored with the spending of money and acquisition of finery. For one thing, it seemed a waste of time to bedeck a country girl in the latest finery only to send her back to the dismal solitude of a

farm for the bedazzlement of bumpkins. Her
heart was no longer in the undertaking. So
she cut the expedition short and the two
women returned to the duchess's home in a
near silence that was not exactly hostile, but
which was far from companionable.

As they entered the foyer, a footman gave
Louise a letter. At first she was thrilled,
thinking it might be a communication from
Trevenaugh, even though there was no reason
to expect him to write her a note. The
duchess was looking at the envelope with
open curiosity.

"A letter?" she said. "But who could it be
from?"

"I shall tell you in a moment, ma'am," said
Louise, opening the seal. She was annoyed at
the infringement of her privacy, but did not
have the courage to make her displeasure
known. She thought fleetingly that whatever
it was that induced the duchess to undertake
her protection—whether kindness or interest—she, Louise, was paying a price for it.
Such thoughts were cut short when she saw
the signature at the bottom of the letter. She
paled and said faintly:

"It is from Lord Castleton, ma'am."

"How interesting! And what does he have
to say?"

Louise read the letter aloud in a low voice
tinged with distaste.

" 'My dear Miss Engleston—my dear

Louise, This is just a note to reassure you of my continued ardor, and of my love and affection for your most delightful person. I know you will forgive my boldness when you understand that I feel it necessary to be bold in order to balance the timidity you displayed this morning in regards to my offer. For it was timidity—even though you don't realize it. Shy little colt! How unknowingly you long for the bridle! With what gentle firmness I shall place that seemingly harsh instrument. It shall be done in such a manner as to perform the most effectively, and to this purpose, my dear Louise, I shall address myself assiduously. On the other hand, if you should not see fit to couple your destiny with mine, I shall pursue the matter we discussed relentlessly. This would prove painful to me, and no doubt to you and to one you hold dear. Let us act in such a way as to make this latter course unnecessary....' "

Louise faltered and dropped the letter. She was very pale and seemed to sway. The duchess, alarmed, helped her to a chair and rang for a footman. When he appeared she ordered tea and waited until it was brought before speaking.

"Well, he seems very determined, doesn't he?" she said.

Louise could only nod. Her heart was still

pounding and fear was sitting in her soul like a tangible, icy presence.

"Ardor, of course, is not to be discounted," continued the duchess, "though his seems peculiarly rural. What is all this talk about putting bridles on horses?"

"He is of the impression that I am like a horse that is to be trained. . . ." said Louise faintly, blushing. She felt humiliated and shamed to have been the object of such attentions.

"Mmmmm. Perhaps he thought to make his point more clearly with a country example since you are from the country," said the duchess musingly.

"My being from the country has nothing to do with it, ma'am. He is a brute, and this is a brute's letter."

Louise spoke with such vehemence that she startled herself as well as the duchess. The latter had become accustomed to meekness in her guest, and was particularly taken aback.

"No doubt, my dear, no doubt," she said placatingly, though she was annoyed at the unwonted sharpness of tone. "It is just possible that he is not a suitable match for you after all."

"It is an absolute certainty that he is unsuitable," said Louise, with more spirit than she had ever mustered. "I cannot understand how this man is allowed to roam free in society."

"He has not really done anything to be locked up for," said the duchess mildly.

"He has threatened my father's life! He has tried to coerce me into marriage!"

"Yes. Well. Reprehensible as these things may be, there is nothing really unlawful, I believe. At most, he can be censured for being ungentlemanly." The duchess spoke thoughtfully.

Louise despaired of making her case to the duchess, and realized with finality that very likely nothing she could say or do would bring that lady to her point of view. She sighed, and sipped her tea with a shaking hand.

The duchess gazed imperturbably out the window, seemingly at nothing at all.

It was into such a scene—on the surface so serene—that Charles introduced himself. He made no effort to conceal his own agitation and unhappiness. He was disheveled and his color was high. His eyes were unnaturally bright, as though they were coated with tears that would overflow any instant. He greeted the duchess with a low bow. She returned a curt nod. He seemed not to notice and turned to Louise.

"We can leave this vile city any time you are ready," he announced.

"Why Charles, what is it?— Have you had news of father?"

Louise could only imagine that he had

found evidence of their father's misdeed and was eager to return to Twelve Elms to be with him. She half rose from her chair.

"I have heard nothing at all from or about father," said Charles with exasperation. Then with guilty sulkiness he added, "It was Mr. Trevenaugh who was to concern himself with father's affairs, if you remember."

Louise silently reproached him for his indifference, but she said gently, "You are very distressed. Has something happened?"

Charles laughed bitterly. Once again Louise noted his tendency to dramatize his emotions. "No," he said. "On the contrary, something has *not* happened." Then he fell silent, but his desire to be questioned was obvious.

After a pause, Louise said, "What is it, then, that has put you into this state?"

"I have been forbidden entrance to Cleo de Merivange's house."

Louise was embarrassed that Charles would even mention the name to her, hoping that his involvement with an apparently unsavory woman could be ignored. But now he had not only mentioned her, he was displaying the power she held over him by admitting the despair she could cause him. She could only respond to the pain that was evident beneath all the fustian of his self-pity.

"I am sorry, Charles. But . . . but perhaps it is for the best?" At a violent movement from Charles, Louise hastened to add, "If I understand the situation properly, it was an affair that had to end someday. It could not last."

"Your sister is quite right," said the duchess, to Louise's alarm. "Such affairs are of necessity ephemeral, and yours had, by all accounts, lasted longer than most." She spoke with the bright interest that Louise had formerly mistaken for kindness. Now she realized that such observations were merely the duchess's method of asserting her control over the gathering. Whatever her motives, however, her remark seemed to placate Charles, even though he continued to stare moodily off into space.

After a pause, he said to the room in general, "I have not given up. I shall not let her toss me aside this way." To Louise the speech sounded hollow.

The duchess replied, "You have the opportunity to do the tossing yourself, you know. She doubtless expects you to moon around her door like a dog for a good many weeks. If you simply stay away, it will be you who has done the discarding."

"But you don't understand, ma'am! I love her!" said Charles, flinging himself into a chair.

"Mmmmmm. Yes, of course. Well, there's nothing can be done about that. Although, if you absent yourself for a few weeks you might be surprised how the 'love' diminishes, without ... flesh ... to give it substance."

"My love for Cleo is not just carnal! It is her spirit, her mind, her very being that I worship."

Louise was embarrassed, for it seemed to her that Charles was making himself ridiculous. Yet she did not know how to stop him. The duchess, furthermore, far from being offended, seemed to relish their dialogue.

"No doubt," she said drily. "Well, now you have the opportunity to refine this sublime love to its essence. Nothing but spirit will be involved. For the time being, at any rate." She smiled brightly at Charles, who seemed to have worked himself into an impasse.

"I really do love her," he said after a pause, and his pain and vulnerability were so apparent that Louise's heart opened to him. She went to his chair and took his hand.

"Charles, we'll go away shortly. This will heal."

He looked as though he might cry, and Louise put her cheek to his and hugged him. The duchess watched them with a brightly interested expression, one eyebrow cocked.

At this point Trevenaugh entered the room. He stopped short when he took in the embracing brother and sister and his observing aunt. Then he cleared his throat and said:

"Good evening."

All three started.

"Why, Henry," said the duchess, "you are just in time to give some manly and worldly advice to this young gentleman. He has, it seems, fallen out of grace with Cleo de Merivange." Her lively good humor was colored with mockery, and she looked as though she expected Trevenaugh to respond in kind.

He, however, turned gravely to Charles, and said, "I am sorry for the suffering this must cause you. But, believe me, for I know so well what I am speaking of, in a month's time you will be grateful that you have escaped."

His voice had more expression than Louise had ever heard in it before, and she marveled that this elegant man, who had seemed so cold and distant, was capable of such sympathy.

Charles seemed to appreciate Trevenaugh's concern also, for, although he said nothing, a current of understanding seemed to flow between them. The duchess took all this in with mild displeasure.

"Well, Henry," she said, "our guest tells me that you have undertaken to save her papa from the gallows."

After a glance at Louise, Trevenaugh answered, "I have undertaken only to right a wrong. And in this I have been, I believe, successful."

The color rushed from Louise's face and

Charles, his grief momentarily dislodged, sat bolt upright. The duchess seemed to accept the announcement with equanimity.

"This is indeed good news," she said, sweeping the room with a pleased glance. "I admit I was somewhat skeptical when I heard of your involvement, but I see I was mistaken."

Trevenaugh bowed ironically in her direction.

"I cannot really take too much credit. I was very fortunate in that I met someone who is in a position not only to exonerate Mr. Engleston, but a great many others as well."

"And who might that be?"

"With your permission, ma'am, I shall ask him to introduce and explain himself." Under the duchess's astonished gaze, Trevenaugh opened the door and signaled.

In an instant, walking slowly, slightly bent from the weight of the large black strongbox he was carrying, and clad in black himself, from his shoes to his jacket, came Nathan Brombedge.

Chapter 12

As a harbinger of salvation, Nathan Brombedge did not cut an imposing figure. He was chalk white, and so weak he could barely support the large strongbox he carried. Little beads of perspiration glistened on his forehead, as though the fact that he was standing was straining his resources to the utmost. Yet there was such an unworldly calm in his expression that the small group was momentarily impressed into a watchful silence—as though waiting for a revelation. None was forthcoming; Nathan Brombedge merely stood with a bemused half smile and calmly regarded nothing at all.

"Well, Henry," said the duchess, nettled that still another unexpected event was taking place under her own roof, "who is this man? Why have you brought him here?"

"May I present Mr. Brombedge, Lord Castleton's secretary . . . and confidant."

"Indeed," said the duchess, and eyed Brombedge with distaste.

Trevenaugh then introduced Brombedge to Louise and Charles, who regarded him with both fear and hostility. Brombedge seemed unaware of the reactions he caused. He acknowledged the presentations with a polite though sketchy nod, then lapsed back into self-absorption.

"Mr. Brombedge," Trevenaugh continued, "has told me a most interesting story—or rather, I should say, several interesting stories. But one, in particular, you will find most enlightening." Here he nodded to Louise. "And the others will serve to dispose of the threat that Castleton has held over your lives for so many years." At a questioning look from Louise, Trevenaugh said, "Yes, he has been a force in your lives at Twelve Elms—greater than you could imagine—for a good quarter of a century. He has made your father's life a miserable burden, and has exerted an influence on the lives of others that has been equally noxious. Lord Castleton has depths of villainy that will surprise all of you."

Brombedge swayed slightly, causing the group to regard him again. Trevenaugh guided him to a chair, in which he sat with the strongbox on his lap.

"Now then," said Trevenaugh gently, "would you please tell these people the same story you told me. Omit no detail, for I wish them to understand, as I have, just how black a personage we are dealing with."

"Very well, sir," said Brombedge, and the room was surprised at the steadiness of his voice. After a hesitation he said, "The story begins, I suppose, when I was a lad on my father's farm in Shropshire.

"I was the third son of seven children. Our farm was prosperous, but certainly not sufficiently so to support so many offspring. My father, however, had the means to furnish me with a fair education—nothing very fancy, but more than adequate for my station in life. Then, through what I thought was the most fortunate stroke that ever befell a lad, a distant cousin who was a barrister wrote to my father asking if he could spare one of his sons, for he wished an apprentice in his profession. There was a chance— though it was not promised—that whomever went would eventually become a partner in my cousin's firm. Neither of my elder brothers had any scholarly inclinations; they were farmers through and through. My father wanted to keep them near him at any rate. I seemed to be the only choice. My father asked me if I would be willing to go to London, and I, who had dreamed of nothing else for months, even years—though I was only fifteen years old at the time—could not contain my joy. Within a fortnight I was settled into my cousin's firm, and as happy as I was ever to be.

"I applied myself, and I was quick, and I rose rapidly both in the profession of barrister and in my cousin's esteem. For the next five years I was like a shooting star—it seemed that I was destined for ever greater things, for I was able, more than able, and agreeable and ambitious." Brombedge's face briefly took on color at the memory of his early triumphs. Then his paleness returned as he continued. "But like a shooting star, my brilliance was short-lived, and doomed to extinction. For I met Lord Castleton.

"I was industrious, and not given to any of the frivolities that London is so full of now, and was then. Yet, from time to time I would indulge myself . . . and seek out a complaisant female companion. It was while I was in the company of one such young female, in an extremely genteel bawdy house, that I was observed by Lord Castleton. He was so highly placed, so far above my station in life, that I didn't even *see* him. So that when he offered to share a bottle with me and my companion, I was at first astonished, then wary—then, to my misfortune, completely flattered and won over. I was to learn later—much later—that it was his way to single out people whom he thought might be of use to him, and that he had heard of my growing reputation as a young and upcoming barrister.

"He was gracious and charming, and I thought that he was impressed by my person and worldly manner. I had never met a member of the nobility before, and here, suddenly, I was drinking with a lord in the most intimate of circumstances. Of course I was foolish not to be more cautious—but I was young, you must remember, and trusting, in spite of my training in caution. Who could doubt the good intentions of a lord?" Brombedge laughed bitterly, then coughed violently for a few seconds. His presence was so assured, however, that no one thought of going to his aid. They sat and watched until the attack subsided and he could continue his story.

"Lord Castleton cultivated me. He sought me out and invited me to places so exclusive I had never even heard of them. I followed him like a puppy. My cousin remarked the friendship, and, though he was older and wiser than I, he encouraged it, for secretly he was flattered that a relative of his and a potential partner in his firm had been taken up by the quality. Castleton, all this while, was trying hard to get me in his debt. I can see this now, though I could not then. He tried to get me to gamble, and when I refused, he tried to get me to establish a liaison with one of the more expensive harlots of the era. He reiterated, time and time again, that if it was a lack of money that was my problem, I had nothing to worry about, for he was my friend, was he not, and what was a friend for, if not to supply funds when needed? But my upbringing had been too solid to be overcome by such arguments, and I resisted his offers. Eventually, I suppose, he would have dropped me as hopeless. But that was not to be, for there transpired the events of a summer night more than a quarter of a century ago.

"One day his lordship invited me to accompany him to Dover for a few days. He said we would have a lark, and that we both needed country air to wipe the city cobwebs out of our brains. He offered, as usual, to pay all the expenses, if money were any problem for me. I suppose that I was piqued at the offer, and also I was, I am sure, afraid of losing a friendship I valued more highly than I knew, by constantly refusing his invitations to entertainment. At any event I agreed to accompany him to Dover the following week. I insisted on paying my own way, of course.

"We set off in high spirits, two young men on a holiday. After we had traveled half a day or so, Lord Castleton confided to me that it was just possible that we might have an adventure during our holiday. He was mysterious and would say no more. I thought he was referring to some amorous dalliance or other, though, and paid no more attention to his hints.

"We arrived at Dover and went to one of the inns. We had dinner ordered in the public room and, when we sat down to eat it, found a very personable, but very tipsy, young man our own age at the next table. Though he was a little the worse for wine, he was a lively and agreeable fellow, and very soon he had joined us. We learned that he had just inherited an estate not too far away, and that he was having his last celebration before settling down with a wife. His name was Tom Engleston."

Louise and Charles gave a start, and Louise found it hard to reconcile the description of the lively young tippler with the sorrowful figure she had last seen at Twelve Elms. Neither said anything, however, and Brombedge continued.

"Lord Castleton proposed that young Engleston join us the following day in an excursion down the coast, as he put it, and Engleston agreed. We parted that night on the best of terms—three young men out on a holiday."

Brombedge spoke the last phrase bitterly, and sat staring into space a moment before continuing.

"The following day we set off, just the three of us, with a huge hamper on another horse, which contained enough food and wine for the day. Engleston was interested in the wine, and began to sample it almost as soon as we had set out. By the time we were well on the road he was already quite tipsy again. I drank sparingly, barely enough to be sociable, and Lord Castleton, I now know, drank not at all. He was always in control of events.

"Our trip began in as lighthearted a fashion as was possible—we were three young men without a care in the world. We traveled along the coast for some time without questioning our destination. Then it occurred to me that we were going rather a great distance just to have a picnic. When I questioned Lord Castleton on this, he put me off with an airy wave of the hand. Engleston was soon too far in his cups to notice, much less question, anything at all.

"So we traveled in this fashion for several hours, until the jaunt ceased to be a pleasure and became tedious. When I protested, finally, that I was hungry and weary, and refused to go any further, Castleton then told me that the object of our excursion had more than just a picnic as its end—that we were soon to be involved in an adventure that we were not likely to forget soon. Engleston was drunkenly enthusiastic. I was apprehensive, though I had no reason to distrust Castleton. It was, I suppose, premonition.

"At any rate, I was not sufficiently alarmed to insist that we turn back. Why should I have been? It was a beautiful day, the sky was a rare blue and the sea was constantly in view. The air was like nectar—and we were young and well favored. . . . It was a glorious day.

"Finally, late in the afternoon, we came to a cove that was all but completely hidden. In fact, it was necessary for Castleton to hunt for several minutes for the opening through the thick growth of bushes that hid it from sight of the road. All the while he was emitting a series of strange prolonged whistles. Soon his whistles were answered by a similar set of signals, and almost immediately afterwards there appeared a most fearsome-looking ruffian, huge and dirty, his greasy hair hanging to his shoulders and a gap-toothed grin slashing his face in half. He greeted Castleton familiarly, and looked us over with insolence. Castleton seemed amused at our reaction (I was probably white and trembling; Engleston seemed momentarily to have sobered up) and made a great show of being intimate with the fellow. Before long there were several other men more or less like the first one—though not so fierce-looking—surrounding us. Castleton told us they were smugglers.

"He also told us that this was the adventure he had planned for us—that we were to cross

the channel to France that night for a ship-
ment of brandy, and return. These fine fel-
lows were to be our guides and rowsmen.
This was to be our lark.

"Now, of course, it sounds mad. But keep
in mind that I was with a lord and a
drunken squire. I was impressed by the
former and rather scornful of the latter because of his drunkenness. Also remember that
smuggling, though as much of a crime then as
now, was still not an unheard-of pastime for
a gentleman—there were many that had their
brandy brought in by their own smugglers.

"In any event, Engleston instantly en-
dorsed the idea, and when I saw how enthu-
siastically he was embraced by Castleton and
taken up by the ruffians, I hadn't the moral
courage to stand up against such opposition.
I agreed."

Louise and Charles had looked surprised at
the description of their father. Brombedge
seemed unaware of any impression he might
be making, and by this time seemed to be
talking solely for his own benefit. He continued in a steady, soft, and almost monotonous
voice.

"When night fell we set off in a large boat
with six oarsmen. Engleston, Castleton, and I
sat in the helm, supposedly to keep an eye out
for the revenue officers. Engleston was still
tippling, and though the air and the adven-

ture had sobered him somewhat, he was once more getting drunk.

"We reached the coast of France, took our cargo, and started our return trip without incident. We had almost reached our own shore again when it happened."

Brombedge closed his eyes and leaned back his head for a moment before continuing. Trevenaugh glanced at Louise, who caught his eye and held it briefly before looking down.

Brombedge continued. "It was a very dark, moonless, foggy night, but our spirits were high—mine were, at any rate—because we had successfully achieved what we had set out to do. And, yes, I was exhilarated because I had triumphed over the law—the law which had been my yoke for the past five years, albeit a welcome and cherished one. Castleton was in good spirits, and Engleston was quite drunk, though he seemed steady enough and coherent. The smugglers—the *professional* smugglers—were rowing with a good will, and we were speeding toward home. Then a challenge rang out over the water.

"My blood chilled. Suddenly there was complete silence in our boat. The men stopped rowing, and we, I believe, even stopped breathing. Then the voice called again, telling us to identify ourselves or we would be shot. The fog and dark were so dense that we could see nothing—nor could they. We remained absolutely still, like animals at bay. Then, terrifyingly, a shot did explode around us. I have no idea how close it came to hitting us, but it seemed the loudest, most frightening sound I had ever heard. We had weapons in the boat, though we had never—God knows—counted on using them. Castleton thrust the guns into our hands with a gesture indicating that we should remain silent. Another shot sounded, and this time I heard, or thought I heard, the bullet whistling overhead. But we remained silent and motionless.

"Then, like a giant beast after its prey, the revenuers' boat came into sight. It was no farther from us than that door. Our terror was unleashed and we fired. Immediately the smugglers took up the oars again and we sped away, but not before we had heard a cry and a curse from the revenuers' boat.

"Miraculously, we outdistanced them. I was trembling in every muscle, and was almost prostrate with gratitude when we reached the shore. We hurriedly hid the brandy, took our departure from the smugglers, and returned to the inn at Dover.

"It was late the next day when we arose and took our first meal. The talk in the public room was of the death the night before of a local lad, not much older than ourselves, the husband of a young wife and father of two

little girls, who had been shot the night before by a band of smugglers. He had been a
popular boy, and there was sincere sorrow in
the inkeeper's manner when he told us about
the killing. I was numb with fear and
despair. Engleston, however, seemed much
worse off than I, because not only was he ex-
periencing fear, he was also in the grips of
remorse. He seemed to feel that he alone was
responsible for the young man's death. After
our meal he withdrew with Castleton and
they remained apart together for the better
part of an hour. I had no idea what they
were discussing, nor did I care. All I
wanted to do was to leave what had become a
hateful place and return to the safety of London.

"Presently Engleston came to me and stiffly
took his farewell. He was, he said, returning
to his estate—his holiday was finished, his
celebration over. I shook his hand and
presumed I had seen him for the last time.

"The following day Castleton and I departed for London. It was during the trip
back that I began to realize what a blackguard he was, and what a situation I had put
myself in by just one moment of folly.

"We—all three of us—had been careful to
avoid any mention of the killing. We were,
after all, gentlemen, and I assumed that there
was no need to discuss the necessity of
silence in the matter. I trusted my compan-

ions. I was correct in assuming that Engleston would be discreet. I was woefully wrong in my assessment of Castleton. For on the road back to London he dropped the first of several hints that were to become more and more insistent and less and less opaque.

" 'It is fortunate,' he said, 'that the local authorities did not learn the identity of the killers of that poor young lad.'

"I thought the remark odd, under the circumstances, but agreed that indeed *we* had been fortunate to escape.

" 'Yes,' he replied, '*you* were fortunate.'

"I assumed, at first, that this was simply a lapse caused by strain. But several times during our trip he made references to the fact that *I* would have to watch my step, *I* would have to be on guard, and so on. Finally I called him to task, and pointed out that *we* had been on an excursion and had committed a crime together.

"He looked surprised and even indignant. And then I realized that I was dealing with no gentleman but a blackguard, for he replied:

" 'But *I* only rode in that boat. *I* did not have any firearm. I did not fire a single shot. I could not have killed that poor young lad.'

"And he was right. Only Engleston and I had the firearms. I began to realize then that it was very possible that I had placed myself at this man's mercy."

Brombedge paused and rested a minute, leaning against the back of the chair with his eyes closed. Then he seemed to shake himself back into the present, and continued his story.

"After we returned to London I decided to avoid Castleton, to sever our relationship. If only I had been able to do so! But he would not allow it. He was like a cat with a mouse, pouncing on me when I least expected it, then withdrawing his claws to give me the illusion of freedom, only to unsheath them again when I began to breathe easier. He would appear unexpectedly and insist we dine together, or visit bawdy houses, to go to the gambling clubs. And always, underneath his pleasant manner, there was the unspoken threat—if I became too independent he had the power to pull me into line. Life became a nightmare for me, for I never had a free moment, never was able to call my life my own.

"I couldn't understand what he wanted from me. Why was he so persistent with his attentions and so dogged with his references to our past folly? Then I learned. For, one day, he informed me that his affairs were becoming so complex as to be onerous, and he needed a secretary. I thought he wanted a recommendation, and I told him that I would give the matter some thought. He smiled—a smile I grew accustomed to as the years proceeded—and said that there was no need to search further, for I, myself, would do very nicely.

"I was shocked. And it dawned on me that this was what he had been working toward. I refused indignantly. After all, my training was drawing to a close, and I was becoming ever more able in my profession. I was outraged that he should value me so low. I was proud, and with justification."

Some of Brombedge's past pride in himself surfaced briefly, and he sat a little straighter and his eye took on a fierce light, which was, however, soon extinguished as the narrative continued.

"But, of course, he won the day. Perhaps I could have fought him, and perhaps won. But I was too fearful of the consequences of losing. It would have been my word against his, a lord and a wealthy one at that. And I could have gone to the gallows if he had prevailed. Who would have believed that such a man as he would have taken off on a smuggling expedition? And it was true that he had not fired a shot and I had. So, after a month's deliberation, after a month's struggle with fear and loathing and despair, I agreed to become his . . . secretary."

Brombedge paused, then continued in his guardedly emotionless monotone.

"It was not too long after I began that I learned that his method of procuring my services was not different from his method of acquiring everything he wanted. He had—has—guile, resourcefulness, and patience. He collects people's weaknesses, pecadilloes, crimes, and mistakes, and this, in effect, makes him their masaer. For he knows how to wait until people are most vulnerable, and then he springs like a spider, his poison being the certain knowledge of a past ommission."

Brombedge looked at Louise and Charles, and smiled with not the slightest sparkle of mirth.

"That is how he entrapped your father.

"I was not aware of the wide application of his method at first, thinking that only I had been the victim of it. But as my duties and responsibilities grew—and as his confidence increased in me—I was made privy to an ever-widening circle of secrets and dealings. I shall never forget the day—after about a year of service—that I was entrusted with this strongbox"—Brombedge indicated the large box he had placed at his feet—"and in it found the confession signed by Tom Engleston."

Louise stirred uneasily, and unconsciously leaned forward.

"This box contains the essence of Lord Castleton's power. He has a remarkable gift for being able to attack when his victim is most vulnerable, and making him do his will, making him produce or create incriminating evidence. Such was the case with Tom Engleston.

"As I said, after the smuggling incident Engleston was shattered with remorse. I saw him and Castleton spend some time together, but thought little of it. Later I learned that Castleton had used Engleston's remorse to influence him to sign a sort of confession. The reason was this: When Engleston heard about the young wife and daughters who had suddenly become a widow and half orphans, he thought he must make restitution. He was, remember, very young, a decent sort, and suffering from the violent effects of the events and the wine of the evening before. It can safely be said, I think, that he was not entirely himself.

"In any event, he signed a note promising to watch over the welfare of the widow and her children from an anonymous vantage point. He would remit a sum each year to Castleton, who would convey it to the beneficiary. It was Engleston who insisted on the formality of a signed note—but I know for a certainty that it was Castleton who put the idea in his head, as well as the idea to state *why* he was undertaking this responsibility. It proved to be the worst error of Engleston's life.

"Each year he made the trip to London with his sum of money—not great, but sufficiently large to put a strain on him, and little by little, the original charitable purpose was forgotten, and the trips became an annual pilgrimage to renew his serfdom to Castleton. The money, incidentally, never did go to the widow, who was not even told of the arrangement. She was a buxom and well-favored lass, at any rate, and did not remain a widow long. She moved from Dover when she took her second husband and we never heard any more of her. Whether Tom Engleston knew this or not, I can't say. I suppose not.

"It would not have mattered if he had known, for after only a few years it was understood that he was paying a token sum to Castleton not to save the lives of a widow and her children, but to save his own. Castleton soon made that clear.

"And that is how Tom Engleston came into the power of Lord Castleton, and how Lord Castleton chose his bride. . . . For, you see, he would never ever take the chance of unleashing his affections on just anyone—it would have to be someone of whom he could be certain." Brombedge looked at Louise.

"And he was certain of you because he knew he had the means of making you do his will completely."

"And he was sorely mistaken," said Trevenaugh. He was calm, but there was a contained anger that surprised Louise. Once

again she met his eye, and once more she had
to deflect her glance.

The duchess stirred impatiently, and said,
"This whole story is preposterous. I do not
know Lord Castleton well, it is true, but I
find it difficult to believe that a man of his
parts should be reduced to collecting scraps
of paper. It makes no sense."

Brombedge looked at her quizzically. "It
makes no *sense*, ma'am, but it happened."

The duchess did not answer, but merely
showed her displeasure by arranging her features into a mask of disdain.

Trevenaugh turned to Louise and said, "I
have taken the 'confession' your father signed
from the box, and will destroy it if you wish.
I would advise you to allow me to do so."

Louise was troubled, and this, mixed with
her gratitude toward Trevenaugh, produced
such a conflict of feelings that she was not
able to answer immediately. The duchess
filled the breach.

"By all means destroy the paper," she said
loftily. "However, the fact will remain that
her father *did* kill one of the King's officers.
You cannot destroy that fact."

There was a pause before Louise said,
softly:

"Yes, you are right, ma'am. I had thought
of that. Father apparently did kill an innocent man, and has gone unpunished for it all

these years. . . . I don't know . . ." and she turned a pleading look toward Trevenaugh.

Charles said, "This was over twenty-five years ago. The whole incident has been forgotten. For God's sake destroy the paper and let's talk no more about it."

Trevenaugh spoke gently to Louise. "I agree with your brother. This all happened so long ago. And your father has paid a terrible price already."

"Not quite so terrible as the young man who was shot down on a foggy sea," said the duchess, with a good-humored smile.

They had all but forgotten the presence of Brombedge. In his small, quiet voice he said, "I think I can dispel any further argument on this matter. Tom Engleston did not shoot the revenuer."

He spoke with such dispassionate assurance that the other people in the room seemed to be calmed by his statement.

After a pause, Louise asked timidly, "How can you be certain of that, sir? You said yourself that you had both fired . . . I assumed that you had both . . . killed the man. . . ."

Brombedge shook his head slowly. "No. I alone killed him. What I omitted to tell you is that much later Lord Castleton confided in me—as though it were the best joke in the world—that the gun that Engleston used had never been fired. In his terror he apparently misjudged the mechanism, and since he was so very inebriated, and since the atmosphere was so charged with fear, he was never aware of his omission. When he heard the gun roar he apparently assumed that he had been responsible."

Louise could not stop the tears of relief and gratitude that sprang to her eyes. She moved to the chair where Brombedge was sitting and took his hand.

"Thank you sir, for your honesty and kindness. I only hope I will be able to repay this debt."

Brombedge said nothing, but nodded slightly in acknowledgment.

"Well," said the duchess, "this seems to be ending very nicely. However, what makes you think that Lord Castleton will stand idly by while you confiscate his property," and she indicated the strongbox at Brombedge's feet, "and agree with you that the whole matter happened too long ago? He can still cause you a great deal of trouble, I believe." She seemed to find the idea quite agreeable.

"I think not, ma'am," said Trevenaugh, more incisively than was his habit. "Another aspect of Lord Castleton's career is just about to come to light. And when it does, he will either have to go into exile—or be killed. In either event he will not be making any more trouble in England for a while."

Chapter 13

Cleo de Merivange was restless and sulky. She was also frightened. It was almost one o'clock in the morning and she had been waiting for Castleton since midnight. She was not accustomed to being made to wait, even by someone like Castleton—who, in turn, was nearly always extremely punctual. She toyed with the idea of retiring and leaving word that she was no longer receiving, but she realized, as soon as she thought of it, that this was a fantasy she dared not act out. She was too frightened of Castleton to risk offending him.

She was also annoyed that she had waited alone—she had expected Trevenaugh to visit her again. She was so certain that he was once more to be a fixture in her life that she had sent young Engleston packing. But there had been no word from him—not even a gift to indicate his renewed ardor. For that matter, not even Charles had come begging to be al-

lowed reentry into her favor. She had begun
to feel the fear that possibly her powers were
waning—that she had lost her ability to inspire desire. One evening alone seemed a
foretaste of doom to Cleo.

Her apprehension had been so great that
she had gathered her jewels, and spent the
time fingering them, calculating their worth,
speculating on how best she could hide them
if need be. She was sitting at her dressing
table inspecting an emerald brooch when a
servant announced Lord Castleton's arrival.
With a sigh of relief and exasperation she
swept the jewels into their case, and turned
toward the door just as Castleton was entering. The reproach that she had prepared died
when she saw his face, and was replaced by
an alarmed:

"Why, Castleton, whatever is the matter?"

He was outwardly as elegantly assembled as
always, but his manner was agitated and his
regard was so wild that Cleo was frightened
for his sanity.

"Have you seen Brombedge?" he asked in a
harsh voice and with a piercing stare that
defied her to lie to him.

"He delivered your message earlier in the
day—that was the only time I have seen
him. . . . Why? What has happened?"

Castleton didn't answer, but groaned and
sat down on the chaise longue with his head
between his hands.

The fear that Cleo had felt became self-interested. Her life was so inextricably linked to Castleton's that any misfortune befalling him would almost certainly deflect upon her. This realization sharpened her second query.

"What's wrong, Castleton? Why are you carrying on this way?"

"Brombedge has disappeared," said Castleton.

Cleo thought of this for a moment, then said, "That is not tragic. At the most it seems to be an inconvenience. I never liked him anyway."

"You fool," Castleton blazed at her. "Brombedge knew *everything*. He has disappeared. And he has taken with him my strongbox—a life's work." Then, in a fit of spiteful fury, he hissed, "Who cares whether you liked him or not? *You* never liked him! Of what importance is it what you like or do not like?"

It was the loss of control rather than the words that further alarmed Cleo. In all the years she had known him, she had never seen Castleton anything but self-possessed. To suddenly see him fling himself about as though he were a thwarted adolescent made her fear for the well-being of their joint ventures.

So it was with genuine concern that she grasped his shoulder and said, "My dear Castleton, calm yourself. This is most unlike you."

He shook himself free and glared at her,

but said nothing. His breathing became more even, however, and as he seemed to be making an effort to control his emotions, Cleo gave hers full rein.

"Does all this agitation mean that Brombedge is aware of what you are up to in France?" she asked, poised to strike if the answer was affirmative, as she knew it would be.

"I believe you mean to say, my dear, does he know what *we* are 'up to,' as you put it, in France. In a word, yes. He does not know the details, but has sufficient grasp of the broad outline to hang . . . *us*."

"I would never have believed you to be such a fool," said Cleo, turning red with anger.

"Be careful of your words, my dear. If I choose, I can throw you to the authorities as a sop, you know. After all, one harlot more or less will not throw the kingdom into consternation. Whereas there is only one Lord Castleton. I would be missed. My disgrace would have reverberations."

"This scheme was your idea, Castleton. It is you who have made the trips to France. You to whom the money was paid. You whom the French know—I have not even yet met the mysterious visitor you promised me a day or so ago. It is you who are the traitor. I have simply been a poor used woman in this whole affair. I have never understood what you were trying to make me do, or why. I have, in short, been innocent. I might be, in some eyes, a harlot. You, however, are a traitor."

"Along with you, my dear Cleo."

"Nonsense. I repeat, I have met none of the Frenchmen, nor have I sold any British secrets."

"You have done worse. You have procured the secrets to be sold."

"Fah. A few stray words from an admiral while resting his weary head on my pillow after a strenuous half hour? Or the flirtatious confidences of a general who is bent on amatory conquest? I passed their maunderings along to my good friend Lord Castleton in all innocence. How was I to know he would hightail it to the Frenchies and sell them what I had told him? I am just a poor girl trying to keep in the good graces of the men who furnish my livelihood."

"You are playing a dangerous game with me, Cleo. Do not, I warn you, force me to bring it to a conclusion."

"That seems hardly necessary. Your former secretary, it would appear, has taken care of that matter for you."

Castleton firmed his jaw and narrowed his eyes. For a second it seemed as though he would strike her, and she made an involuntary move away from him. He restrained himself, while never once taking his eyes off her face.

After a pause he smiled and said: "It is foolish in the extreme to argue this way. Our well-being is based on our continued mutual trust. Under the strain of the moment we have forgotten ourselves and bickered like children. Now we are calm again. We must figure how best to save the situation."

"Save the situation! My dear Castleton, now we have to save our lives!" Cleo spoke with controlled vehemence.

"Quite right, my dear, to think in such drastic terms. Although, you know, we have no certitude that Brombedge has absconded with the purpose of exposing . . . us. He may merely want money from us."

Cleo tossed her head with such scorn as to indicate the observation was beneath comment.

"But," continued Castleton, as though he had not noticed, "in the event that exposure was on his mind, we must be prepared. Now, as I see it, we can go to France until the whole affair is forgotten. Or we can try to find Brombedge and . . . persuade him to follow a more reasonable course. Actually, it was in hopes of pursuing the latter alternative that I came here. I thought you might know of his whereabouts."

"What you thought was that I might be in partnership with him, you mean," said

Cleo. "I know how your mind works. Your every action is coated with suspicion. What I do not understand is why this admirable caution was not applied to your own secretary."

"He has been my secretary for twenty-five years," Castleton flared. "Furthermore, he had every reason to avoid incurring my resentment. I can ruin him. I cannot understand his behavior." Castleton was almost petulant in his annoyance.

"And what about your marriage?" asked Cleo relentlessly. "Are you taking Miss Engleston with you to France, or are you going to suggest a long engagement?"

"That is no concern of yours," said Castleton coldly.

"On the contrary, my dear Castleton, everything about you concerns me now. After all, your behavior has put my life in the balance. . . . Well, what about the marriage? Are you going to abduct Miss Engleston, or will you have her join you of her own free will?"

"There will be no marriage," said Charles Engleston, as he stepped into the room.

Both Cleo and Castleton froze, with looks of astonishment on their faces. Castleton was the first to recover, and his reaction was to dart glances around the room, seeking for a means of escape. Cleo's recovery was more languid.

"Why, Charlie," she said after a pause, and with a forced laugh, "how you startled us. How did you get in?"

"That was easy enough. I should know my way around here by now," Charles said with exaggerated bitterness. "But we can't waste any time. I've come to tell you that everything is known about your dealings with the French. His secretary"—he indicated Castleton with a scornful gesture—"has told everything to us and is now telling it to the Prime Minister. They will be searching for you tomorrow morning, or maybe immediately. I've just come from them. Cleo, you will have to leave the country. I've come to take you away." He said the last sentence with bravado, but there was an underlying note of pleading.

The statement seemed to act like a stimulant to Cleo. Her back straightened and her color glowed. Her eyes sparkled, and her smile was slow and seductive.

"Charlie. You would do that for me?" she said.

Charles looked at her with longing and, instead of answering, seized her hand and kissed it. With her other hand, Cleo caressed the nape of his neck. She flashed a triumphant glance at Castleton, who was watching the scene with speculative detachment.

"The young man is right," he said coolly.

"We should leave immediately. Be ready in a half hour's time. I shall have the coach here and we shall leave for Dover."

Charles turned an inflamed glance at him. "I am here to save Mademoiselle de Merivange. You, sir, who are responsible for her troubles, will bother her no more."

Castleton merely raised an eyebrow and smiled into the middle distance. It was as though Charles had not spoken.

"Tell him to leave, Cleo," Charles said imperiously. "What he does to save his own skin is no concern to me. But he shall not touch so much as a hair of your head."

Cleo was once again in control of the situation, and she relished her role. She glanced with amusement at Castleton, and said, "So, Castleton, I have a champion."

"Indeed you do, ma'am," he replied. "But by all accounts a rather impoverished one. I do not envy the style you will cut in Paris if you are to rely on this young man's funds. Of course," he added ironically, "you can always support the two of you with your own assets."

Charles turned a furious stare to Castleton and said, "I shall find the means to support Mademoiselle de Merivange. Perhaps we shall be poor, but we shall have each other."

"Touching sentiment," said Castleton affably, "but it does not seem to have impressed the lady."

"Certainly Cleo did not look pleased. Her mouth was set in a grim line and exasperation creased her forehead.

"I will not be fought over like a bone desired by two dogs," she said.

"My dear Cleo," said Castleton, "please note that I am not fighting. I am merely describing a reality. You will, of course, do as you please. I am leaving now and shall pass here again in half an hour. If you wish to accompany me you will be waiting in your foyer. If I do not find you there I will understand that you have chosen the path of disinterested love."

Castleton bowed and walked from the room, leaving an annoyed Cleo looking after him.

Charles took her hand again. She allowed him to hold it for an instant, then withdrew it impatiently.

"I must get ready, Charlie," she said absently.

Charles asked, softly, and pleadingly, "Is there anything I can do? Shall I . . . shall I go to find the carriage?"

"No, Charlie. I shall go with Lord Castleton," she said calmly, and walked into her dressing room.

Charles sat on the chaise longue and stared at the floor. He stayed in this position until Cleo returned to the boudoir in a green velvet traveling outfit. She was carrying her jewel case. Though she had had to dress herself without help, she looked as beautiful as she had on the first day they had met. The dress brought into even greater prominence her green eyes. And her bearing had a gallant edge to it, sharpened by adversity, it seemed, that enhanced her appeal.

She cast a distracted eye about the boudoir, as though checking to see whether anything had been forgotten. Then she seemed to notice Charles and smiled at him rather wryly.

"I must go downstairs now," she said. "Castleton meant what he said. He would leave without me if I'm not there when he comes."

They descended the stairs together, silently. Then Charles, unable to restrain himself, said:

"Cleo, don't go with him. Go with me. Now."

She looked annoyed, as though at an interruption by a clumsy servant, and did not answer.

"He doesn't love you," Charles persisted. "I do. I *will* take care of you. You'll see. Please come away with me now." His voice was almost a whine, and desperation was in every gesture.

Still, Cleo did not answer him, but moved silently toward the door leading to the street. Charles grabbed her arm and turned her toward him.

"Let go of me, Charlie," she said, her eyes

narrowed with anger. "And stop babbling to me about love."

Her tone was so cold and decisive that he dropped her arm. She stepped through the door into the street and he followed her. In the distance he could hear wheels and horses' hooves ring through the early morning silence. Then he saw the coach and four horses coming down the deserted street.

In one last, desperate effort he said, "If you insist on going with Castleton, then I will accompany you. I will make it all right with him—"

With quiet exasperation she turned to him, just as the coach pulled up to her door, and said, "You don't understand, Charlie. I simply can't afford you anymore."

She swiftly stepped into the waiting coach, the door was closed by the outrider, and the driver snapped his whip. The coach clattered off into the darkness.

Charles, his face burning with rage and humiliation, leaned against her door, and did not even watch it go.

Chapter 14

There was the usual morning bustle in the duchess's household as Louise descended to breakfast, dressed in a simply cut light woolen dress of dark blue. She was all ready. Her two battered old trunks were packed, and the two others furnished by the duchess to accommodate her new finery were also ready. She was pleased to be returning to Twelve Elms—but she was melancholy to be leaving London. Though her exposure to the luxurious life of the city had been brief, it had been seductive. She was going to miss the elegance, beauty, and pomp. Specifically, she was going to miss Trevenaugh.

She had admitted it to herself the night before, after he had extracted the confession from Brombedge and then had gone with him to see the Prime Minister in order to give warning of Castleton's treachery. Her first glimpse of Trevenaugh—the elegant London buck—had been deceiving. Or rather it had been incomplete. For though the elegance was real, it was only the veneer for a strong will and a masterful nature. He had proven to be resourceful, courageous—and most surprising and endearing to Louise—compassionate. His embracing the difficulties that had beset her family had won her completely—or had she already been won before? She no longer knew. His quiet sympathy for Charles, particularly, had been ingratiating. All these feelings had been building gradually, unbeknownst to her, until last night they forced themselves into her consciousness, and she admitted to herself that she had never met anyone like Trevenaugh, and it was unlikely that she ever would again. She sensed that there were probably even more, and deeper, attractive hidden recesses in his personality that would remain forever mysterious to her. She had lain awake most of the night exploring them in her imagination. Now, descending to breakfast, she allowed a cloud to wander across her face as she reflected that she would never have the occasion to test her imagination against reality, would never know what Trevenaugh thought of children, would never learn whether he was kind to the poor, would never see his behavior toward animals. . . . She sighed softly and entered the breakfast room.

The duchess was already seated at the table, a plate piled high before her.

"Good morning, my dear," she said as she zestfully speared a kidney on her fork. "I trust that you passed a peaceful night, now that all your troubles are over." She chuckled.

"Very well, thank you, ma'am," said Louise, and she went to the sideboard where the same lavish display of food had again been created.

"And so now you will be leaving us," said the duchess, with a most insincere sigh of disappointment. "Our lives shall be the drearier for your loss."

"That is very kind of you to say, ma'am," said Louise quietly, but without much conviction. She felt uneasy about the hostility of the duchess, and had not reconciled herself to it. She wondered if there was something she might do to retrieve the good will that had seemed to mark their relationship initially. When she had needed a friend the most, the duchess had turned on her for no cause that Louise could discern. It had been a saddening experience. She decided that there was nothing she could do now except to behave in such a way as to render the brief remainder of her stay as pleasant as possible. So she helped herself to breakfast and settled down at the table across from the duchess with an agreeable smile.

"I have tried to thank you before, ma'am, but you have always insisted that you have not acted out of kindness. Now I do wish to say that, whatever your motives, I am most grateful for the assistance you have given me and my family."

"My dear," said the duchess, "I will accept your thanks if it will make you feel better. Though I believe it is not very astutely placed. It seems to me that whatever gratitude you have should be lavished on my nephew." She smiled, with a faint streak of maliciousness showing through.

"Indeed, you both have been most helpful," said Louise, blushing.

"No, my dear. Henry has been helpful. I have simply permitted you to share something I already have, namely my home and my money. It has cost me no effort. I have seen to that."

Louise acknowledged the truth of the statement by remaining silent. She decided that any effort on her part to win the duchess over would be futile. She was about to launch an innocuous conversation on the weather, something to fill the time in as bland a way as possible, when Charles entered the room.

His appearance drove any idea of bright chatter from Louise's mind, and caused even the duchess to gape a moment, for he was as haggard and worn-looking as a man twice his age. Great black circles encompassed his eyes, and his usual brilliant complexion had turned grey. Most frightening was the dead, lusterless expression he surveyed them with. His clothes were carelessly thrown upon his body and his whole attitude was one of despairing indifference.

"Good morning," said the duchess after a pause, during which Charles had stood in the doorway, seeming to regard them from a great distance.

"Good morning," he replied quietly, and in his tone and attitude there was more sorrow than in all his posturing of the preceding days.

Louise longed to go to him, but he seemed so determinedly withdrawn that she feared any display of emotion would offend him. She said, as calmly as possible, "Good morning, Charles. Are you ready to leave?"

"Yes," he replied listlessly. "We can leave whenever you like." He sat at the table without taking any food, and stared into space.

After a brief silence, the duchess said, "You don't seem to be yourself this morning. Are you feeling well?" She spoke with a hostess's superficial concern.

"I was out late last night," he replied indifferently, without looking at her. His indolence seemed to pique the duchess into solicitude.

"Perhaps," she said, "you should eat something."

Charles glanced languidly at the sideboard, then went to it, took a plate and placed random tidbits on it. He brought it back to the table and began mechanically eating.

It was his response to the duchess's suggestion that alarmed Louise more than anything else—the old Charles would have rebelled at any recommendation, and, even if starving, would not have given in. His compliance indicated great stress.

She decided that at all costs he must be retrieved from his lethargy, and was trying to find some scheme that would jolt him back to liveliness, when Trevenaugh entered the room. All other thoughts fled when Louise saw him. She looked at him openly and frankly, convinced that this was the last time that she would ever see him. She felt a physical pain in her chest when she realized this, and her breath came short and more quickly. His eyes met hers, and for once neither of them glanced away, but held the look for what seemed a very long time. It was interrupted by the duchess, who was observing them.

"Well, here's Henry. The savior—of the Englestons *and* of England herself." Her tone could not have been more affable.

"Good morning, ma'am," said Trevenaugh quietly, taking his eyes from Louise and bowing to the duchess.

"Here we are all together again, just as we were last night—only that dreadful little man in the black suit is missing. I presume he will be along shortly?" she asked with irony.

"No ma'am, Mr. Brombedge is furnishing more information to the Prime Minister's secretaries, after which I have arranged for him to go to the country to rest. He is not well, as you must have noticed."

"So he is to be the instrument of vengeance against Lord Castleton and Cleo de Merivange."

"He is furnishing information on their activities. However, they have fled England, presumably to France. So there is no question of vengeance at the moment."

"Fled, have they?" asked the duchess. "Curious that they should have known their scheme was discovered. How ever can that have happened, I wonder?" She smiled at Charles, who ignored her and continued eating.

"It is no matter," said Trevenaugh. "The important thing is that Castleton's fangs have been removed. He cannot harm innocent people or his country now."

"What I have not understood is why he should have undertaken such activity in the first place."

"According to Mr. Brombedge, ma'am, Lord Castleton was—and is—exceedingly fond of being in control of both men and events. He lusted for power the way other men lust for women. His obsession with it is inordinate. It finally has done him in."

"Mmmmmm. For the time being at least," said the duchess. "Ah, well. And now you have come to say farewell to our guests, who will be returning to their country haunts."

Trevenaugh turned to Louise and smiled slightly.

"I have come to . . . speak to our guests, certainly."

Louise's heart beat faster. She looked directly at Trevenaugh again, with her new-found boldness, and this time did not blush.

"Perhaps, Miss Engleston, you will be good enough to take a stroll in the garden with me?" he said.

"Excellent idea," said the duchess. "We could all use some air. Let us by all means proceed to the garden." She smiled broadly at the other three people in the room.

With admirable control Trevenaugh merely nodded and offered his arm to Louise, who took it without a moment's hesitation.

The duchess looked exasperated. Then, putting her pique aside, she swooped upon the startled Charles and said, "Come, come, now, we are going for a turn in the garden. The air will do you good."

Obediently he got to his feet, offered his arm, and followed Trevenaugh and Louise through the French doors into the garden beyond.

Once in the small garden, Trevenaugh had a great deal of privacy in spite of the duchess's proximity. The meandering paths were only wide enough for one couple, and by keeping his voice low he could avoid being overheard. But now that he had achieved this privacy, he seemed at a loss as to what to do with it. Louise was little help. So they strolled in uneasy silence for a few turns, while behind them the duchess's chatter was unceasing. Finally, Trevenaugh cleared his throat and said,

"So you are leaving. You have had a very short stay."

"It has not seemed short. So much has happened in these last few days—can it only have been four days ago that I came to London?"

"It must have been a very unpleasant experience to seem so long."

She paused before answering. "It has not all been unpleasant. I was frightened and worried, it is true." Then, much more softly, she added, "But there will be many cherished memories of this visit."

"Ah," he said. "Perhaps you will share them with me?"

"Surely," she said, so softly as to be almost inaudible, "you must know that you figure prominently in them."

Trevenaugh was silent for a few steps. Then he said, "It is your candor, your lack of artifice that I have found so attractive.

Your answer once again underlines this quality."

Louise could think of nothing to say. She was suddenly short of breath, and thought for a moment that the tension in her breast would make her lose consciousness.

Then Trevenaugh continued, "I shall be distressed if this should prove to be our last meeting. I hope that you will give me permission to visit with you at your home, to meet your father, and to see you in your own surroundings."

Louise breathed deeply to still the beating of her heart. Then she murmured, "Nothing would make me happier than the knowledge that I shall see you again."

Trevenaugh hesitated and seemed short of breath. Still they strolled slowly. After another turn he said, "Perhaps . . . perhaps . . . you will entertain . . . will permit me to be so bold—" He stopped as though suffocated by his own words. He took a deep breath. "Perhaps you will allow me to offer you my name in marriage."

Louise felt the tenseness in his body as she faltered on the path, and leaned against him for an instant. She was afraid she would faint, and she put her hand to her breast as though to still her heart. She did not look at him, but stared at the path before her as they continued to stroll slowly and carefully, for all the world like two people who have nothing but trivial matters to chat about. When she found her voice she said:

"You have honored me, sir, with your request—"

"No, it is you who honor me by hearing it," Trevenaugh interrupted, as though he were frightened she would come to too rapid a decision. "Please do not feel compelled to answer me straightaway. I do not wish to force you . . . I respect—I love you too much to try to coerce you into a marriage against your will—"

"Oh, sir, how can you think it would be against my will?" Louise was so moved that her voice betrayed her agitation. "There is nothing that I want more, that I *could* want more, than to be your wife."

They paused an instant and looked at each other, then quickly turned their eyes back to the path. Trevenaugh gave a sigh of relief and pressed her arm nearer to his body. The gesture was so slight as to be almost imperceptible, but the duchess, behind them, noticed it and said loudly:

"Enough of this walking, now. We mustn't tire our guests before their long journey, Henry—which I'm sure they are eager to get under way."

She led the compliant Charles back to the dining room, followed by Louise and Trevenaugh, who walked slowly and with increasing physical awareness of each other.

As they entered the room, the duchess said to Louise, "My dear, *how* I am going to miss you. But of course we shall write often to each other, and certainly, we shall see each other from time to time." She spoke with blatant insincerity.

Louise was hurt by the underlying coldness of the duchess's dismissal, and was not sufficiently adept to conceal it. She replied, "I am truly sorry to have caused you so much trouble and disruption of your household. My whole family owes an enormous debt to you for your hospitality."

"Yes. Well."

Charles startled everyone by speaking. "I think we had best be on our way, Louise," he said drily. He turned to Trevenaugh. "Thank you for your help." Then to the duchess. "Thank you for protecting my sister. Come, Louise, everything is in the carriage. There is nothing more to keep us here." He spoke with brusque finality, and started moving toward the door. Louise, with a lingering glance at Trevenaugh, started to follow him, when a footman entered.

"There is a Mrs. Hartshord to see you, ma'am," he said to the duchess.

"Mrs. Hartshord?" said the duchess. "I know no one by that name. Whatever it is she wants, I am not at home. Send her away."

"Oh, that is my aunt, ma'am," said Louise.

"Indeed," said the duchess glacially, "and what would *she* want with me?"

"Perhaps," said Trevenaugh with a slight smile at Louise, "we could find out by inviting her in."

There was no need to issue an invitation, for at that moment a formidable figure in brown silk, bristling with self-importance, swept into the room, and after a cursory glance around it, fell into a low curtsy before the duchess and said, "How do you do, Your Grace."

The duchess regarded her with extreme distaste for an instant. Then, without a word, she turned and glided from the room, leaving Mrs. Hartshord curtsying into empty space.

"Good morning, Aunt," said Louise timidly.

Mrs. Hartshord, her dignity imperiled by her odd stance, rose to her full height and said testily, "Well, Louise, I have rushed back from Bath when I received your singular request for shelter, given at such short notice. Then my servants told me you were staying with the Duchess of Bledrough," and she looked around, as though she hoped that lady would somehow reappear, "and I came immediately to fulfill my duties as an aunt." She was extremely put out.

"I regret the trouble I have caused you—" began Louise.

"Miss Engleston had to come to London on

short notice and was unable to send you word sufficiently in advance," said Trevenaugh smoothly, amiably, and with tact, "so my aunt was fortunate enough to act as her hostess during her all-too-brief stay."

When Mrs. Hartshord heard Trevenaugh refer to his "aunt" she looked at him with interest.

Louise said, "May I present my aunt, Mrs. Hartshord. This is His Grace, the Duke of Wickenshire."

Mrs. Hartshord's eyes took on renewed fire when she heard the title, and she would possibly have executed another curtsy had not Trevenaugh forestalled her by taking her hand and saying, "It is a pleasure indeed to meet the aunt of Miss Engleston. I am looking forward to a long, long acquaintance with your family."

Mrs. Hartshord seemed more than mollified at this information, and even regarded Louise with a new air of interest.

"Well," she said, "and I am very pleased to make *your* acquaintance. And now, my dear niece, I suppose you will be coming home with me?" she added affably.

"Thank you so much, Aunt, but no, Charles and I are leaving this morning for Twelve Elms."

"So soon? I cannot understand such a short visit."

"The next visit," said Trevenaugh, looking

at Louise very intently, "the next visit you make to London will be much, much longer."

And he took her arm and led her to the carriage.

Reading Fit For A Queen

QUEEN-SIZE GOTHICS offer the very best in novels of romantic suspense, by the top writers, greater in length and drama, richer in reading pleasure.

☐ A GALLOWS STANDS IN SALEM—
A. M. Bretonne   00276-X   1.25

☐ AULDEARN HOUSE—Barbara Riefe   03194-8   1.50

☐ THE ABBOT'S HOUSE—Laura Conway   00328-6   1.25

☐ AN ADOPTED FACE—A. S. Carter   00272-7   1.25

☐ ANCIENT EVIL—Candace Arkham   08559-2   1.25

☐ ANGELICA—Jean Anne Bartlett   08579-7   1.75

☐ BLACKTHORN—Arlene Fitzgerald   03203-0   1.50

☐ THE BRIDE OF CAIRNGORE—
Jean F. Webb   00376-6   1.25

☐ CASSIA GREAT HOUSE—Iona Charles   08557-6   1.50

☐ THE COUNT OF VAN RHEEDEN CASTLE—
Scott Wright   08474-X   1.25

☐ THE COURT OF THE THORN TREE—
P. Maxwell   00592-0   .95

☐ DARK SIDE OF PARADISE—
Jo Anne Creighton   00390-1   1.25

☐ DARK TALISMAN—Anne-Marie Bretonne	00240-9	1.25
☐ A DELICATE DECEIT—Susan Hufford	00398-7	1.25
☐ THE DEVIL'S GATE—Arlene J. Fitzgerald	03178-6	1.50
☐ THE DEVIL'S SONATA—Susan Hufford	00340-5	1.25
☐ DEVIL TAKE ALL—A. Brennan	00612-9	.95
☐ DRAW A DARK CIRCLE—Iona Charles	03191-3	1.50
☐ THE DREAMER, LOST IN TERROR— Alison King	00356-1	1.25
☐ FOOLS'S PROOF—A.S. Carter	00261-1	1.25
☐ THE FOUR MARYS—Rinalda Roberts	00366-9	1.25
☐ GRAVE'S COMPANY—S. Nichols	00252-2	1.25
☐ GRENENCOURT—I. Charles	00264-6	1.25
☐ THE HARLAN LEGACY— Jo Anne Creighton	03206-5	1.50
☐ THE HEMLOCK TREE—E. Lottman	00235-2	1.25
☐ INN OF EVIL—J.A. Creighton	00224-7	1.25
☐ ISLAND OF SILENCE— Carolyn Brimley Norris	00411-8	1.25
☐ ISLAND OF THE SEVEN HILLS—Z. Cass	00277-8	1.25
☐ KEYS OF HELL—L. Osborne	00284-0	1.25
☐ THE KEYS TO QUEENSCOURT— Jeanne Hines (Empress)	08508-8	1.75
☐ THE LAZARUS INHERITANCE (Large type)—Noel Vreeland Carter	00432-0	1.25
☐ THE LEGEND OF WITCHWYND (Large Type)—Jeanne Hines	00420-7	1.25
☐ LET THE CRAGS COMB OUT HER DAINTY HAIR—J. Marten	00302-2	1.25
☐ LUCIFER WAS TALL—Elizabeth Gresham	00346-4	1.25
☐ MIDNIGHT SAILING—S. Hufford	00263-8	1.25
☐ THE MIRACLE AT ST. BRUNO'S— Philippa Carr (Empress)	08533-9	1.75
☐ OF LOVE INCARNATE—Jane Crowcroft	00418-5	1.25

Buy them at your local bookstores or use this handy coupon for ordering:

ALL TIME BESTSELLERS
FROM POPULAR LIBRARY

☐ THE BERLIN CONNECTION—Simmel	08607-6	1.95
☐ THE BEST PEOPLE—Van Slyke	08456-1	1.75
☐ A BRIDGE TOO FAR—Ryan	08373-5	2.50
☐ THE CAESAR CODE—Simmel	08413-8	1.95
☐ DO BLACK PATENT LEATHER SHOES REALLY REFLECT UP?—Powers	08490-1	1.75
☐ ELIZABETH—Hamilton	04013-0	1.75
☐ THE FURY—Farris	08620-3	2.25
☐ THE HAB THEORY—Eckerty	08597-5	2.50
☐ HARDACRE—Skelton	04026-2	2.25
☐ THE HEART LISTENS—Van Slyke	08520-7	1.95
☐ TO KILL A MOCKINGBIRD—Lee	08376-X	1.50
☐ THE LAST BATTLE—Ryan	08381-6	2.25
☐ THE LAST CATHOLIC IN AMERICA—Powers	08528-2	1.50
☐ THE LONGEST DAY—Ryan	08380-8	1.95
☐ LOVE'S WILD DESIRE—Blake	08616-5	1.95
☐ THE MIXED BLESSING—Van Slyke	08491-X	1.95
☐ MORWENNA—Goring	08604-1	1.95
☐ THE RICH AND THE RIGHTEOUS —Van Slyke	08585-1	1.95

Buy them at your local bookstores or use this handy coupon for ordering: